MW00916650

JACK

AND THE

JUNGLE LION

STEPHEN JARED

JACK AND THE JUNGLE LION

First printing, 2010

Copyright © by Stephen Jared 2010

Cover art by Paul Shipper 2010

Book design by Paul Shipper

For further information about the author visit –
www.stephenjared.com

For further information about the artist visit –
www.paulshipper.com

For further information about the book visit –
www.jackandthejunglelion.com

ISBN: 978-0-557-50893-8

A Romance of Adventure

for Tracy

INTRODUCTION

Everyone liked Jack Hunter. The whole world knew him—or thought they did. His movies were marvels of light-hearted heroics, quick wit, and charm, each almost perfect portraits of the dashing star himself. Scandalous shenanigans have been well documented by Hollywood enthusiasts, but there are many Jack Hunter stories that have never been told. Perhaps that task—now that so much time has passed—should fall to me. For once upon a glamorous time, I knew him well. My father and he shared many of Hollywood's best years, and at some point I began asking questions. I found myself stunned by the stories I heard. Finally, with his family's kind permission and with tremendous enthusiasm, I began writing them down.

The best story might be how Jack met Max—Maxine Daniels. Everyone knows they married and shared many decades together. But only a few people today know how they came to meet.

Under most unfortunate and extraordinary circumstances Jack Hunter and Maxine Daniels found themselves on the run from headshrinkers in the Amazon. Hard to believe, I know. And yet, it's true. During the course of this hair-raising adventure, or misadventure, as the old actor might have referred to it, Jack revealed himself to be something quite different from the swashbuckler he had been pretending to be in pictures. Everything changed for the star at that point, never to be the same again. If you had met him, he would have told you that for him what could have ended in unspeakable horror turned out to be, remarkably, the best thing that ever happened.

And so, daunting as the task has been, I have tried to reflect the lightning-fast wit, the debonair voice, and the old-Hollywood charm of Jack Hunter. Here is the first in a series of stories as personally recited to me by the star himself when I was a very young, always eager listener …

CHAPTER ONE

This tale—how Jack met Max—started one morning in 1937, when Mr. Quigg, Jack's butler, entered an enormous bedroom carrying a tray of cola and aspirin. After quietly placing the tray on the nightstand, Mr. Quigg drew the curtains, flooding the bedroom with sunlight. Crumpled up in the bed, half-dressed from the night before, the sprawled-out figure of Jack Hunter began to stir.

Eyeing the bed, Mr. Quigg clasped his hands at his back, raised his chin, and cleared his throat. "Eh hmm ..."

Jack moaned. Moments later a second grumble was heard. Finally, Jack pulled his head from the pillows and raised a hand to block his bloodshot eyes from the sunlight. "Oh, God! Have you no mercy? Mr. Quigg! No! That light's killing me!" A thought suddenly occurred to Jack Hunter, inspired by the circumstances in which he presently found himself. "You know, I think I could've played Dracula. If I wasn't so good-looking."

"And if you could act."

"Ah ha! Very funny, Mr. Quigg."

"Your aspirin and cola are beside you, Mr. Hunter."

"Very good." Jack swung his aching feet to the floor, hunched over the nightstand, and then knocked back his best hangover remedy.

"It is precisely nine thirty in the morning," Mr. Quigg offered. "Which means you are two hours late, exactly as you requested."

"Well done. Where's Mrs. Hunter?"

"Mrs. Lomond has been up for some time and is presently downstairs, waiting impatiently."

"Perfect."

Mr. Quigg was never caught smiling except with his eyes, an ever-so subtle expression of amusement Jack witnessed often.

Meanwhile, on the first floor of Lomond Manor, trouble brewed. Jack's wife, Theda Lomond, addressed her staff in a tone condescending and much too familiar to all who knew her. Theda was mostly famous for her melodramatic portrayals of aristocrats in extravagant silents from more than a decade earlier. In other words, she played herself (and was her biggest fan). However, by 1937 the once bright star began to fade, and she didn't like it one bit. "Fools! Imbeciles!" She had a habit of spontaneously barking these words even when alone, releasing them from an inner dialogue she tried keeping to herself.

"I examined the mop in the utility room," Theda proclaimed to her staff. "It was dry, which means it has not been used today, correct?"

Staff members awkwardly looked to each other without moving their heads.

When speaking, Theda used the crisp diction of one brought up by a troupe of British thespians—though she was not. "Well? Does someone have an answer?" Theda's penciled eyebrows reached for the ceiling as Mr. Quigg stepped down the grand stairway with Mr. Hunter's emptied tray.

Suddenly, with slick dark hair perfectly parted, lean figure magnificently suited in a tuxedo, "Action Jack" came to light at the top of the stairs. "Darling! Don't move a muscle!"

Theda put a hand to her forehead. "Not again," she complained. "I'm tortured by childishness."

Jack flew onto the banister. He slid down the stairway, passing Mr. Quigg in a flash. Nearing the bottom, he took to the air again. A chandelier rattled, supporting his weight as he swung forward, let go, and dropped to his wife's feet.

Continuing with his Saturday-matinee heroics, Jack grabbed Theda's waist, pulled her to him, and declared, "Never fear, darling! Your knight in shining armor is here!" With his remaining free hand, he used his finger as a pistol, pointing at the smiling staff.

With delight, the smiling staff members applauded, slapping their hands together in a state of rapturous awe. Mr. Quigg approached, allowing for a tiny sparkle in his otherwise dry eyes.

Jack stepped forward and bowed. He then extended his arms out, presenting himself for further adulation, when one arm knocked a tray of steaming coffee down the front of a female staffer. She screamed—loudly.

Embarrassed, Jack watched her dash away then pulled a clip of cash from his jacket, peeled off a few fat bills for the poor girl and handed them to Mr. Quigg. "Buy her something nice while I'm gone."

"Good luck to you in South America, sir."

*   *   *

Jack and Theda occupied the rear passenger compartment of a splendid 1932 Maybach limousine. It took a good deal of time to reach Santa Monica's airport from Beverly Hills—but what a luxurious stretch of road!

Theda refilled her champagne glass, never spilling a drop, returned the bottle to its pure silver ice bucket, and turned her heavily powdered visage to Jack.

Through an open window, the handsome star enjoyed the air rushing in his face, the sight of passing palms and mansions; he looked happy—until his wife furiously rolled up his window.

"Jack, you must tell me. How was she?"

"How was who?"

"Last night."

"Last night?"

"Please don't treat me this way, Jack. I need to know."

"Uh … I'm a little perplexed."

"I can't bear to speak her name. Please be smart for a moment."

"Oh … You mean Lombard? Carol? The screening? Last night?"

"Yes! Keep stabbing my poor heart, why don't you!"

"Uh … She was terrible. An awful performance."

"You lie."

"You know, you've been in a bad mood since we saw her in *Hands Across the Table*. That was two years ago."

"She stole my career."

"Before that it was Jean Arthur in *The Ex-Mrs. Bradford*."

"How dare you."

"Claudette Colbert in *It Happened One Night*."

Unable to withstand another second of such abuse, Theda threw her champagne at Jack.

"Thank you, darling," Jack responded, pulling a handkerchief to gently dab his face. "You know, you've been angry for ten years."

"I'm an artist. You've no idea the madness that brews inside my soul."

Jack quickly replied, "Well, I wish there was something I could do about that."

"There is."

"What's that, dear?"

"When the photo hounds begin shooting at us, you can try kissing me without upstaging me as you've done in the past."

"I don't understand."

"Allow my face to be seen when you kiss me good-bye. In other words, kiss me on the cheek farthest from the camera."

"Swell."

*   *   *

Santa Monica Airport seized a patch of high land just shy of the Pacific. Small planes casually took the air, ripping the blue skies slowly and noisily. The little airport catered to the local film community and to the studio holding Jack Hunter's contract, his dramatic departure for South America cried out for publicity. "Picture this!" Louie the studio boss bellowed at Jack weeks earlier. "Screaming kids! Screaming twin engines! The whole world'll be going nuts for the great Jack Hunter!" Louie always spoke with the jubilant animation of a desperate salesman; nevertheless, Jack liked the idea.

A stage had been assembled and microphone set up, awaiting parting words and questions from an adulatory press. Parked near the stage, a beautiful Ford Trimotor angled toward the sky, the bright sun bouncing off its silvery skin. Newsreelers readied themselves to capture obligatory footage.

There was a lot of restless energy, people kicking at the pavement, checking watches, and smoking cigarettes, until finally—far behind schedule—Jack and Theda arrived. Fanfare erupted. A crush of movie crazies, waving issues of *Screenland* and *Movie Mirror*, lunged toward them. The driver gently pressed their luxury limo through mass adoration and parked by the stage.

Exiting the front seat and squeezing through the mayhem, the driver rounded the lengthy motorcar to Theda's door. Excitement intensified as he opened the door and Theda appeared.

"Theda, my dear!" Louie shouted over the ruckus, stretching toward her. "Theda, my stunning goddess! How good of you to come!"

As the driver hurried to Jack's side, anticipation mounted over the already frenzied state. Young fans chanted, "Action Jack! Action Jack! Action jack!" Decibels rose higher yet as the driver's hand reached for the door. It opened.

Out stepped Jack Hunter. Just then all attention shifted from Theda's mask of bashfulness to the king of boyish vigor. Flashbulbs popped. Piercing cries clamored for his attention. Patient in the face of so much chaos, Jack smiled affably, warmed by his success. In fact, he absolutely loved it.

While shaking hands and signing autographs, Jack tenderly pushed his way to the stage. Louie kissed Theda's gloved hand and escorted the glamorous star, making a big show of his chivalry for the cameras. Eventually, the studio boss and silent film queen flanked Jack at the microphone.

The crowd quieted.

"Why isn't the lovely Theda Lomond traveling with you?" one snappy reporter demanded to know.

Jack scratched at his forehead and half-smiled. "The location's authentic this time. We'll be roughing it in the jungle. My wife's a city gal."

Theda stole the microphone, adding. "As well, there are film roles that I'm considering."

"What can we expect from the new picture, Jack?"

Noticeably annoyed by the lack of interest in her, Theda stepped aside. Jack quipped, "My films aren't exactly translations of Russian literature, and to that I say, thank God. This will be the seventh picture I've done with director Hal Hartford. It'll be in the same ballpark as the others—"

"Only better!" Louie interjected, unable to help himself.

Without much notice, the Ford Trimotor's door flew open. A pilot with a slightly tubby frame observed the spectacle, removed his cap, and rubbed his potato-shaped head. Despite his impatience, he had an endearing face and quick comical eyes.

"You're known for your appreciation of beautiful women, Jack. How are you going to get by without your wife for so long?" another reporter asked with a mischievous grin.

"My obligation down there is to save the world from evil, and I guess I'll just have to try and stay focused on that."

Without warning, the Ford Trimotor's engines rumbled to thunderous life. Cameras turned to the readied airplane as youngsters again chanted, "Action Jack! Action Jack!"

Jack looked to Theda. Aware of the microphone amplifying his voice, he said, "So long, darling," and then kissed her in the manner she had requested, his handsome face farthest from the flashing bulbs.

Theda too played her part melodramatically, full of fake tears and batting eyelashes. "Oh, Jack!" she cried. "Must you really go?"

Jack pat his heavy heart, waved to all, and bounded off the stage and into the Trimotor. "I'll be back!" he shouted.

The Trimotor stood more than twelve feet tall, with a wingspan of seventy-seven feet. It had a reliable, rugged appearance. Inside, Jack met two pilots. The first was an older, square-jawed man with a firm handshake. "Press make you nervous, Mr. Hunter?"

"No, my wife does."

"Ha!"

The second was the tubby fellow in coveralls. After removing his cap and jamming it under an arm, he shook Jack's hand till his jolly cheeks jiggled. "Pleasure to know you, Mr. Hunter!"

"That's very kind of you. And your name is?"

"Clancy. Yessiree. Glad to make your acquaintance. I'm the copilot. And this," he said, motioning to the square-jawed man, "is Captain Horrigan."

"Well, it's a privilege to meet you gentlemen."

"Thank you, sir. Now, if you'll excuse me …"

While Captain Horrigan climbed into the cockpit, Jack and Clancy noticed Louie ogling the Trimotor's interior. "Decided to come with me, Louie?"

"The Ford Trimotor's a beautiful plane, Jack."

"Captain calls her his old Tin Goose," Clancy cut in.

"That so? The Tin Goose."

"After we return, Captain Horrigan and I'd be glad to take you up, buzz around over the Pacific some afternoon."

"Oh! I would love that! I'd be most indebted to you. And, believe me," Louie exclaimed with a wink. "The head of a movie studio can pay a debt in a lot of interesting ways."

"You wouldn't owe a thing," Clancy offered.

Louie stepped away from the plane. "Good luck, Jack!" he shouted over the engines. "Hit one out of the ballpark for us!"

The door closed and Clancy secured the lock. To Jack he announced with a friendly smile, "Guess we'll be off."

The copilot joined his captain while Jack strapped in. As the deep rumbling of motors intensified, they were finally ready. With a sudden lurch forward they raced down the runway and swooped skyward, far up into the blue. After climbing high over the Pacific, they turned south, gaining speed, traversing the old globe's latitude lines.

CHAPTER TWO

The Trimotor flew low, bouncing through turbulent skies. Their course remained due south. With cotton-stuffed ears tempering the shrill cry of the engines, Captain Horrigan and his copilot Clancy patiently covered long distances with short conversation. To battle the cold air, they put on leather jackets and rubbed their hands together for warmth.

On his right side—out of his captain's view—Clancy had hidden a bottle of whiskey. He reached for it occasionally, dropping a few splashes into his coffee mug.

In the passenger section of the airplane, Jack found it hard to get comfortable; he too was cold. With eyes closed, he rubbed his arms and fidgeted in his seat, until finally he stood. Searching a cabinet for a blanket or anything with which he might warm himself, he found nothing. Tired and frustrated, he turned back to his seat and observed a most unexpected sight: two hands, very small ones, clutched the top of a chair toward the rear of the airplane.

"Hello."

Caught, a little boy lifted his mischievous face.

While he knocked on the cockpit door, Jack's gaze remained in the direction of the little boy who now returned to hiding. "Hmm ... A rascal, I suppose."

Appearing from the cockpit, Clancy said, "At your service, Mr. Hunter."

"We've got a stowaway."

"Stowaway?"

Then a second child came into sight. A handful of years more mature than the first, this new discovery was a girl. She wore thick glasses over big blue eyes and had some separation between her front teeth.

"Hey, what's going on here?" Jack wondered aloud.

"Oh, that's just Max and the kids," Clancy explained, dismissing all sense of alarm. "There was a problem with their school schedules. They couldn't make it down as early as everyone else. So Max convinced someone to let them fly down with the last trip, which is this one for you."

"Who's Max?"

"She's the animal trainer on the movie."

"She?"

Rising from a deep sleep, Max became visible, stretching and yawning huge like a lion. "Yahwwwa! My goodness! When do we land?" She wore a tightly fit houndstooth riding jacket and white scarf. Soft curls cradled a handsome, luminous face.

But it was something within her, something unseen, that caused Jack's heart to leap, and he just knew he would never be the same.

"I think she's their aunt or something," Clancy prattled on with no further attention paid to him. "Not sure what the situation is there."

So spellbound was Jack that he neglected to notice the boy walking toward him. "Can I have your autograph?" the little one asked.

Clancy patted Jack on the shoulder, said, "Let us know if you need anything. We seem to be making good time," and returned to the cockpit.

Jack looked down finally, found the boy's face staring up at him. "Hmm? Sorry? Oh, hello, fellow. An autograph, you say?"

"Yes, sir."

Jack knelt to the boy. "An autograph? An autograph, you say? Okay. Sure. Why not? Do you have something to write with?"

"No."

"Oh, I see."

"Tyler …" Max called to the boy as she approached. "Tyler, I'm sure Mr. Hunter would appreciate not being disturbed."

"Actually," Jack responded. "I love signing autographs." He stood tall, met her face-to-face, eyes sparkling with interest. "I'm Jack Hunter."

She recognized the flirtatiousness in his warm brown eyes. At first, she remained silent, steadied a cautious expression on him. Then finally she offered her name. "Maxine Daniels. Friends call me Max."

"Pleasure flying to South America with you."

"Yes, well, pretend we're not here." She held up a confident smile and, with an unusually tomboyish voice, spoke rapidly. "We don't want to be an intrusion. Feel free to practice lines or do push-ups—whatever it is you do."

"Oh, no, I'm happy to have company. You don't need to hide back there."

"We weren't hiding. We were sleeping. We were waiting a long time, and it was getting a little boring."

"Unfortunately, my delay was necessary," Jack lied. He knelt again. "Tell you what, Tyler, before this adventure is through, I promise we'll track down something to write with and I'll get you that autograph."

"Can I have one too, Mr. Hunter?" The girl stepped forward, clutching a hardback Emily Brontë with both hands.

"Sure."

"This is Lindy."

"Hello, Lindy. Say, are you two ready for a *real* adventure?"

"Yes," the children answered together.

"Good to know. If we meet up with any pirates or anything, just stay by my side. I'll protect you."

"How about that, kids? Say thanks to the nice swashbuckler."

"Thanks nice swashbuckler." Tyler held the screen hero in his bright eyes, awestruck by the sight of him in person.

"Say, you know," Jack continued with the boy "it occurs to me that you look just like I did when I was your age. Any idea what you might want to be when you grow up, son?"

"I told my Auntie Max that I want to be like you."

"That so? Like me, you say?"

"But she said you probably have a fat head and are full of hooey."

"Oh, she's probably right about that," Jack conceded as he stood.

"Not because you're in the movies," Tyler went on, now looking up at him. "She says all men are fatheads."

"I see."

"Tyler, dear, it's not good to say everything that races through your mind."

"I often do the same."

"Well, Mr. Hunter, before you start, maybe we should return to our seats."

"Oh, ah, very well," Jack muttered. "I'll get those autographs to you. Before we say so long for good, I'll—I'll get them to you."

"That would be very considerate, Mr. Hunter. The children would appreciate it."

"Yes. Well …"

Jack sat down again, as they did, feeling bewildered. Maxine Daniels puzzled him, made him feel strange. He almost convinced himself she didn't feel a surge of excitement from his presence, which would make her remarkable. She talked funny too. The pleasant tone in which she spoke directed her listener away from any possible offense to be taken from her words. What was that about, he wondered. Jack closed his eyes in an effort to sleep but now felt even more uncomfortable than before. He pulled a flask from his tuxedo jacket, took a very serious sip from it, feeling a highly unusual slip in confidence.

*   *   *

Much time and several stops had passed. The constant cold blue of the sky had become tiresome. Clancy snored. His still hidden whisky bottle lay dry. A particularly loud honk woke him a bit. He mumbled something, sang a soft unrecognizable tune, and peacefully drifted off again.

At that moment, Captain Horrigan removed a steady hand from the controls, and looked at it, confused. He winced suddenly, violently, knotting the lines in his face.

"Aah!"

His jaw locked. His left hand abruptly covered his heart, gripped it, while his right hand shook over an array of levers, gauges, dials and switches. He struggled to speak, to communicate to Clancy, but couldn't.

He slumped forward—dead!

The weight of Captain Horrigan's lifeless body pushed the steering wheel forward, driving the nose of the Trimotor down. The airplane raced toward the ground like a rocket. The sound was deafening as all three engines screamed and the metal frame clattered.

Clancy awakened. He reached for and lifted the bottle to his face. Then it hit him: the bottle was empty. Far worse, they were flying like a fastball toward the hard surface of the planet. And had little time left.

"Uh-oh."

In the passenger area, Jack shouted. "I think something's wrong!" He removed his seatbelt, pulled on the velvet curtains covering his window—and froze at the sight.

Max rushed past him, entering the cockpit. Her discovery beat the worst of expectations. Through the windows, she saw green earth rising in a hurry to meet them. Clancy stood over his captain's seemingly sleeping body, shaking him. When he looked up with swirly half-closed eyes, Max shrieked, "You're drunk? What's the matter with him? The nose has to come up!"

She grabbed Horrigan. "He's ... Oh, my gosh!" Moments from crashing, she pulled the pilot's body off the wheel. "Help me!"

Clancy hiccupped and seized the wheel with her. Together they pulled as hard as they could, struggling against their dangerous speed. With barely seconds to spare, the Trimotor's nose lifted, coming within a couple-dozen feet of the dark forest below. They leveled off.

Jack finally charged through the cockpit door. "Everything okay?"

Clancy pointed through the windows, slurring. "Mr. Hunter, the ocean's green an' lumpy!"

Max clobbered poor Clancy with her high volume inches from his ear. "That's the jungle, you old fathead! You idiot! You lush!" She pivoted to Jack. "We got two pilots! One's dead and the other's drunk! Get in here and help me!"

"I don't know how to fly a plane!" Jack's eyes widened at the sight of Captain Horrigan slumped to the floor. "Oh, my gosh! Is he really? Really ... I mean, is this? This can't be happening!"

"All I know is this wheel thing has to be pulled back and stay back or we go down!" Max lifted her heels to the control panel for leverage and more strength as she pulled the wheel toward her.

"Maybe there are instructions on how to fly this thing!" Jack frantically searched for some.

"They're probably in the same place as the instructions on how to get you to suggest something smart!"

"Hey, I'm trying to help!"

Clancy's eyes had fallen completely shut. "I c'n fly the plane. I c'n fly the plane. Doo'nah worry."

A narrowly perceptible stretch of open land suddenly presented itself ahead of them. Max pointed. "There! That looks like a place to land!"

"You're going to land?"

"We're going down sometime! This may be our best shot!"

"Well, wha—wha—what if we crash?"

"Mr. Hunter, get in the back and tell the kids to get down and put their hands over their heads."

He hesitated.

"Do it now!"

Clancy sank to the cockpit floor as Jack rushed to the back. Max focused, eased the wheel forward, gently. Her breathing quickened as their altitude dropped. She resisted the urge to pull back up as their time had run out—another few seconds and they would surely overshoot the opening in the forest below. Easing the wheel farther forward, she sent them barreling toward the treetops.

Tyler and Lindy watched Jack shuffling awkwardly toward them, stumbling this way and that. He muttered incoherently, trying to speak, but words came out jumbled. Jack crouched, and the kids knowingly copied his position. Lindy protectively, lovingly, sheltered Tyler in her arms.

"How do I work the brakes?" Max shouted at Clancy within the cockpit.

"The—uh—whatchamacallit thingy—"

Max yanked on a gearshift, praying she had done the right thing. "Hold on!"

A heavy wing was clipped and taken by a high palm. The Trimotor spun, dropped, and skipped. They lost the other wing. The body of the Trimotor slammed nose first into a tree with a sudden earsplitting crash of metal and glass.

A rush of debris caught up with the wreckage like a powerful wave. Very slowly, dust settled over what remained.

CHAPTER THREE

Lindy wiped a tear and squeezed her brother as he lifted his head from beneath a busted seat. Their immediate feeling was relief—they were still alive. They turned to the action star who lay facedown on the battered floor of the airplane.

Jack moaned, sniffled a little bit, until he looked up and saw that the children were fine. Rising to his knees, a smile broke on his face, and they fell into his arms.

"You all right?" Jack asked. Responding to their nods, he sighed, "Thank God."

Tyler spoke weakly. "Auntie Max …"

Jack turned to the closed cockpit door, wondering. Worry gripped each of them as they recalled the calamitous impact. Jack stood. His tattered tuxedo, combined with his always-impeccable posture, belied the vulnerable look on his face. He swallowed hard, stepped forward expecting heartbreak and then—

Something thumped. The cockpit door burst open. Max appeared, rattled but smiling at the sight of her worst fears abated.

"Auntie Max!" The children jumped, elated.

Stumbling past tight embraces, out into the passenger area, came Clancy as well, mumbling. "Got walloped about pretty good in there."

"It's extraordinary," Jack said. "We all made it!"

"Well … almost," Clancy added, lifting his eyes to Jack and sounding nearly sober.

"Horrigan. Yes," Jack said, acknowledging the tragedy. "Heart attack must've got him. Poor soul."

"Well …" Clancy unleashed a troubled breath. "I think we'll have a hard time getting this bird back in the air."

"Ha! Brilliant deduction."

Clancy winced at Max's venomous snap. His head fell to his chest, weighted with shame. "Sorry, ma'am." He removed his cap, rubbed his head, and quietly cursed at himself.

"Wait a second," Jack interrupted, eyes growing larger. "I just thought of something. We've got to get off this thing before it blows!"

Alarm galvanized them again!

Jack grabbed at the door, rattling the stubborn handle, but it appeared they were trapped. "A fine patch of daisies this is," he snarled.

Circling him, the others grew increasingly anxious. Jack stepped back then launched himself, full body, into the door but it didn't budge.

"Release the safety lock," Clancy helpfully suggested.

"Huh?"

Clancy hit the latch, unlocking and opening the door, inviting a wave of dense heat, sunshine and jungle sounds.

"C'mon!" Jack bellowed. "Women and children first! We've no time to lose!"

Max dropped from the Trimotor to the forest floor. Pivoting back, she helped the children down and, with Jack and Clancy on her heels, hastened into the thicket as fast as her legs would allow.

Waving his arms, calling his trustees deeper and deeper into the jungle, Jack warned, "Get down! Get down!"

Gaining a good distance from the crash, they leapt behind a cluster of bushes. Crouching for a long time, sucking in soggy air, they listened—and waited. Certain an explosion was imminent, Jack covered his ears and squished up his face. Much time passed. Soon, their stretched-tight nerves relaxed.

Max stood. "I suppose there is a chance, however remote, that the airplane is not going to explode."

Jack straightened himself, removed his fingers from his ears. Baffled, he said, "Hmm … probably snuffed out by all the moisture in the air. We are in the rainforest, after all." Suddenly, the soft ground behind him collapsed. His arms flailed wildly as he fell back. "Aah! What the—"

Clancy cried, "Mr. Hunter!"

Jack's pained body lay twisted in a torturous position, at the bottom of a deep ditch, cleverly masked with palm fronds.

"You okay, Mr. Hunter?"

"I've been more comfortable, believe me." Irritated, the handsome star struggled to his feet. "Some silly animal hole or something," Jack guessed. As he moved to tidy his hair, he saw that his arms had been pricked by hundreds of thin sharp sticks. His back and legs were covered too.

"That's not some animal hole." Max spoke with a troubled voice, which gradually grew into a roar. "Get out of there! Hurry!"

Frantically, Jack scrambled out and brushed his body free of sticks. Max helped, battering him with panic-stricken swings.

"What? What is it?" asked Jack, shrinking from the blows.

Max stopped, scanned the dim depths of the jungle, and said, "We must be in Jivaro territory."

Everyone trembled, unsure.

"Is that a bear or something?" Jack wondered.

"How do you feel?"

"I don't know—itchy. Why?"

"The poison must be too old."

"What? What do you mean 'poison'? What are you talking about?"

"The Jivaros aren't bears, Mr. Hunter. They're people. And this isn't an animal hole—it's a trap! They put poison at the ends of these sticks!"

Turning white as a sheet, he slapped at his torso and limbs for more sticks, and removed his jacket and fiercely shook it. Perspiration dripped from his forehead.

"All right, just calm down," Max said soothingly.

"Calm down? Calm down? I'm not used to these kinds of circumstances! You'll have to excuse me if I'm a little hysterical!"

"The poison's old. If it wasn't, you'd be dead by now."

Tears welled in the actor's eyes. "I feel funny," he said in a high-pitched, breaking voice.

"I'm telling you, you're fine."

"Well, that's great," said Jack, nearing a state of emotional collapse. "I've got a few more minutes to live till something else happens! Our plane crashed! We're lost somewhere in South America! I fell in a poison-stick pit!"

Max came very near to his face and spoke in a fast whisper. "Mr. Hunter, for the sake of the children, would you stop blubbering?"

"Huh?"

Tyler and Lindy watched the silver-screen hero with long, disappointed—even shocked—faces.

Jack swallowed hard, blinked tears from his eyes and sniffled. "Darn these allergies," he lied. "I'm allergic to—um—to—um—"

"Here's a hanky for your nose," offered Max.

Clancy kicked at the dirt, stuffed his hands in his coveralls, and dropped his head again. "This is all my fault. I've always made a mess of things."

Max whirled round to him. "We're gonna need you to suck it up too, flyboy. No turning yellow. It's against the rules. No feeling sorry for yourself, either. Do we have a map?"

"Uh—well—yeah, but I have no idea where the YOU ARE HERE part of it would be."

"I vote we try to get to the movie location," suggested Jack.

Max removed the white scarf from around her neck and dabbed her forehead with it. The heat was beginning to take its toll. "That's a great idea," she said. "Why don't we all pull out our magic lanterns and see how many wishes we have left."

Rocking back and forth on her heals, Lindy asked, "What are we gonna do?"

"We should head for the coast," Max decided, checking the angle of the sun against the horizon. "It's our best shot at finding a village, maybe someone who has a boat or a plane." Her humorless gaze dropped down to the pit. "We should move quickly. What do we have to eat?"

"Candy bars and beans."

Jack turned his nose up at the copilot. "I can't eat candy bars and beans!"

"I thought you were the one who could save us from pirates?"

Feeling awkward, Clancy attempted to assuage Max's harsh sarcasm. "We also have a few canteens of water, ma'am. It should be nice and cold and refreshing," he promised.

"Well, God's not gonna reach down, pick us up, and take us somewhere. Let's go," said Max. "Our chances depend on our speed. I'm sure we'll make it out of here just fine."

The stranded five started back to the Ford Trimotor. Far off in the jungle, a pack of howling monkeys erupted in excitement, causing heads to turn. Nearby, frogs resumed croaking and braying after having been hushed by the crash. Everything seemed alive, sluggishly moving, creeping.

Clancy rushed alongside Max. He tried apologizing. "I know I caused all this, ma'am. I want you to know, it was never my intention to—"

"You set a real fine example for my children. I hope you think about that."

Max hurried on as Clancy's footfalls slowed. Jack, having witnessed the exchange, offered the copilot a reassuring pat on the back.

There could be no comforting Clancy, though, as he once again turned his eyes up to the wreckage. Pieces of the Trimotor stretched over a hundred yards. Their survival had been miraculous, and they all knew it.

Max was the first to climb back inside the compacted body of the plane. She reached around to help Tyler and Lindy aboard, aided by a heave-ho from Jack. Clancy took up the rear.

The majority of what remained was of no use to them. Clancy picked up a blanket—first thing—and took it into the cockpit. Max rummaged through a canvas bag of supplies.

"Maybe we could turn this airplane into a boat," Jack said, making conversation.

"That's the dumbest thing I've ever heard."

"I'm just suggesting—"

"Maybe we could use your empty head as a flotation device. How about that for a suggestion? Would that work? I think it probably would."

"You know, it's not going to help us if you're going to be snapping at everyone."

"Mr. Hunter, you'll discover I'm not a woman who can easily be told what to do."

"I'm sensing that."

From the canvas bag, Max removed the heavier items she determined to be unnecessary, like a hammer and a Spanish-language dictionary. She sifted through spools of fishing line, sunglasses, and a bottle opener to find candy bars, beans, and soda cracker packages.

Clancy emerged from the cockpit without the blanket, wiping tears, punctuating his reappearance with a weighty sigh.

"Are you sure we shouldn't bury him?" asked Jack.

Slinging the supply bag over her shoulder, Max said, "We're a little pressed for time."

Sniffling, Clancy nodded in agreement, murmuring, "He would have wanted it this way. He loved this old Tin Goose. God rest his soul."

Jack allowed a moment then said, "Miss Daniels found some supplies. Do we have any weapons?"

Clancy, collecting himself further, asked, "You mean like a gun or a knife?"

"No, like slingshots. I thought we could protect ourselves from the poison-pit makers with slingshots."

"We'll be fine. We won't be needing any weapons," Max said definitively.

With the profound shock of their predicament passing, Tyler and Lindy's energies resumed to something closer to normal for their age. Together, they leapt out the door, returning to the rough terrain, the undergrowth, the humidity, and the insects.

Clancy followed, having grabbed the water canteens.

"We won't be needing any weapons? Really? Wish I could share in your sunny outlook, angel," Jack said to Max.

Quietly, so the others couldn't hear, Max responded, "There are headhunters around this part of the Amazon. We could have our heads lopped off, shrunken, and sold in a shop. But I'm not going to say that in front of the children. As best as I possibly can, I'd like to protect their innocence."

Jack watched Max hop from the plane and march off. "Lovely," he mumbled before trailing after her.

Determining which direction to go by the sun, they left the open area of the forest, trudging through darkness created by a canopy of tall trees. Clouds of gnat swarms shifted fast in the air despite the enervating tropical heat.

Tyler asked, "What are we gonna do when it gets to be nighttime, Auntie Max?"

"Just stay by my side, sweetheart."

As their journey into the grim, green jungle began, Clancy removed his cap, wiped his sweating face with it as he took one final look back at the wrecked Ford Trimotor, which tragically became his captain's tomb.

CHAPTER FOUR

"*Captain Gunner and the Lost City of Gold. Revenge of the Python Men.*" The marooned maintained their westerly direction while Tyler rattled off names of pictures that starred his movie hero, Action Jack Hunter. "*Fighting Ace and the Spell of the Voodoo Women.* And the one with that jewel that would get real bright ..."

"*Desert Paradise of Doom*," Jack recalled.

"No, it was *Treasure of the Sahara Sky.*"

"It was? Oh, that's right."

"You were in the desert in Africa. Don't you remember?"

"Or the ever versatile Culver City. Sure, I remember. Oh, the fun we had."

The rainforest offered enchantment and fear with every step. A lovely looping whistle from some bird species battled vocally against an ear-splitting screech from another.

Max led with a stick, swatting spiderwebs and leaves, pushing through a tightly sewn patchwork of trees. Bats swooped overhead. Falling arrows of sunlight caught flying things and tossed shadows.

"You were looking for the jewel so you could marry the princess," Tyler said, aiding Jack's memory.

"But then he didn't want to marry the princess," added Lindy.

"Hold on a minute," Jack muttered, eyeing the little girl and putting a momentary end to their incessant slog. He removed the flask from his jacket pocket.

"Don't you think we've had enough trouble from that?" questioned Max.

Jack knelt to Lindy's skinny legs, which had become scraped from thorns and thick leaves. He cupped a hand, poured whiskey over it and then rubbed it against her sores, causing her to flinch. "Just relax. Think good thoughts," he said softly. "This may sting, but it'll keep those bites and cuts from getting infected."

"Very thoughtful of you, Mr. Hunter."

"Thank you, Mr. Hunter."

"Please, call me Jack. Calling me Mr. Hunter makes you all sound like my wife's staff." Lastly, Jack removed his tuxedo jacket and wrapped it around Lindy's waist. With the sleeves tied behind her, the back of the jacket now protected the front of her legs.

Lindy's blue eyes looked up at Jack through thick glasses. "Do you remember the scene where you danced with the princess in that ballroom in Cairo?"

"Sure."

A toothy smile flashed. "That was my favorite part."

"I'd be happy to show you a few steps once we've returned."

Lindy bit her lower lip, embarrassed, said, "Okay, thanks," and hurried to catch her brother and Auntie Max as they continued.

Jack whispered to Clancy, lifting the flask, "Saved a little nip for you in case you need it, chief."

"I'll be fine." The copilot smiled appreciatively. "Thanks just the same."

Through dim light and dense foliage, they carried on. Each step forward was placed with care. The unremitting croaks and warbles of critters became less frightening after a time, overpowered by the vastness of the great Amazon.

Max, still leading them, stopped.

Dread gripped her followers as they witnessed the sudden end to her movements. "Auntie Max?"

Her head remained still, angled down at the path before her. She said nothing; fingers stretched wide, palms aimed behind her, frozen.

"Auntie—"

Without words, Jack and Clancy ambled past Tyler and Lindy, peering over Max's shoulder. What they saw resembled the root of a giant tree stretched across the path. However, absurdly, this root moved steadily like a slow-going locomotive. The sight was a mystery to all, except Max.

"Uh—that's a snake."

"It's too big to be a snake." Jack swallowed hard; his breathing quickened, tensed. The behemoth reptile produced only the faintest rustling of leaves as it traveled.

"It's an anaconda."

Clancy pulled his cap over his sweat-drenched mug while his wild, disbelieving eyes tried grasping the size of the slithering monster. "It's moving, and there doesn't seem to be an end to it."

"They can grow up to thirty feet long."

"Let's hope this guy just ate a flagpole and has no room for dessert."

"We should be okay. They usually drop from the trees when they attack."

"Comforting." Jack looked up, and something heavy fell on his nose—a raindrop. The unexpected splat caused him to clutch his throbbing heart and slip into a state of teeth-chattering hysterics. "Aah … Aah …"

"Shh!"

Rain dripped, pattering on leaves, rapidly strengthening to a drizzle. They lost sight of the fiendish snake as mud swallowed their feet and dark clouds roamed over the high treetops. Thunder rumbled in the distance.

"Jeepers creepers! Where's King Kong when you need him?"

"Mr. Hunter, please calm down."

They raised their voices above the sounds of the torrential rain now hammering them. Massive quantities of water came sheeting down through high swishing and swaying trees. They were soaked and—as night falls fast in the jungle—would soon be in total darkness.

*　　　*　　　*

Fortunately, Clancy had a lighter. The five misplaced souls surrounded a crackling fire. Walls of darkness had closed in around them, creating a more intimate world. Flames lit branches and the ragged trunks of nearby trees. Faces glowed bright.

The storm swirled elsewhere.

Tyler and Lindy slept—she with a hand over her book, he curled up on his side. Max and Clancy sat talking over the fire. Jack was on his back, but his eyes remained attentive, aimed at the night sky sparkling through a black veil of trees.

"My sister didn't make it through Tyler's birth," Max explained to Clancy, in answer to an inquiry about the children. "And their father was a womanizer even when he was married to my sister. I could see it was difficult for him to juggle children and girlfriends so I offered him a solution. He agreed without hesitation."

"Doesn't sound like a very nice man."

"Not many can look beyond their own selfish interests."

"He's awful lucky to have someone like you come in and sacrifice for his irresponsibility."

Her tough voice softened. "I thought it was a sacrifice at first, but these kids have made me feel like the luckiest person on the planet."

"Well, they're great kids despite their father."

"The funny thing is if you met their father, you'd probably like him. The world is a playground to him. He's a dashing, smiling, charming fellow."

Clancy's eyes rolled back as he chuckled and said, "Sounds like Jack Hunter!"

The handsome—though disheveled—movie star slowly raised his head from the jungle floor.

"Er—sorry, Mr. Hunter," Clancy muttered with some embarrassment. "Thought you were asleep."

"A person's reputation doesn't always reflect the person," Jack stated simply.

"Have you ever cheated on your wife?" The blunt question came from Max, asked with squinting eyes and a deepening tone. She took on the air of a Spanish Inquisitor interrogating a fifteenth-century heathen.

Somewhat awkwardly, Jack replied, "Uh—have I eaten all my life? The answer to that would be yes."

"Ah, I knew it! You're a big fat phony. And you have the audacity to be smug about it."

"You don't understand."

"What's to understand?"

"My wife doesn't care."

"All women care, Mr. Hunter. You'd have to be inhuman."

"Some marriages work better as professional partnerships rather than romantic ones, especially in Hollywood. When a star marries another star, you've doubled your press."

Clancy curiously asked, "Are you saying Clark Gable and Carol Lombard—"

"No. I'm explaining to you that my wife doesn't care."

The animal trainer and the Tin Goose copilot looked at each other. Quickly adjusting to Jack's sad revelation, Max dismissively said, "Still, that's no excuse."

During the uncomfortable, pondering moments that followed, Jack noticed Clancy fidgeting—jamming hands under armpits, shaking, scratching his head, tugging on clothes. Jack had witnessed these symptoms in others, recognized them as side effects of heavy drinking abruptly cut off.

Despite his distractions, Clancy resumed his conversation with Max. "How'd you know about those sticks in that hole in the ground?"

Jack dropped back again and closed his eyes.

"My father was an anthropologist—"

"Boring!" Jack exclaimed, interrupting.

Max snapped, "You don't even know what it is."

"Do too."

"What is it?"

"A scientist."

"A scientist who studies ...?" Max let the question linger, incomplete.

"Yes."

"My question is not to ask whether the scientist studies or does not study. Its 'what does an anthropologist study?'"

"Ants."

"Very good, Mr. Hunter. I underestimated you. My father actually won an award for a paper he once wrote comparing the brain patterns of ants to actors. Guess which species proved to be the more intelligent?"

"I can't hear you anymore because I'm sleeping."

"Maybe since you're sleeping you'll actually stop talking."

"So," Clancy cut in, "your father was an anthropologist?"

"Yes. I think we could have a more intellectual conversation if we pretend Mr. Hunter has gone to sleep. Let's try ignoring him and I'll tell you about my father. He had been here before, you know. Several times. He used to tell my sister and me the most amazing stories about it. My familiarity with the Amazon through him is what got me this job. There's a story I told to the Hollywood movie-studio people that my father told us. It involved a pig-like creature that lives around here. They call it a capybara. One day, my father and his team of researchers happened upon a lagoon and were about to wash off. Well, out of the jungle waddled this happy-go-lucky, fat creature. It passed right by them and swam into the lagoon. They thought it very cute. But once it reached several yards out, all of the sudden the water around it erupted. The capybara screamed bloody murder as it was being devoured.

Within seconds only the skeleton remained. It had been attacked by a school of piranha. Without realizing it, that pig saved my father's life and the lives of his team. My father cried over the death of that animal."

"It must've been a horrible thing to witness."

"The studio people I told found it hilarious. They giggled till they almost fell on the floor."

"Some men do stupid things to hide the way they truly feel."

"Then they're cowards. I don't know how their wives put up with them. I'd rather be alone than be with a coward."

Bothered, Jack remained still and quiet, eventually succumbing to uneasy dreams.

CHAPTER FIVE

As the new day's heat cut into the forest, steam climbed the trees and dissipated in the higher skies. Exotic bird squawks contributed to the chorus of hungry grumbles from jungle critters everywhere.

The terrain swelled. Ascending high hills and sharp ridges, the crash survivors found less oppressive humidity; however, much of their progress on this second day had been from climbing and, without proper nourishment, all were tired. Jack tried keeping their spirits from darkening with talk of his film career.

"One of the movies I made took place in the jungles of New Guinea. These evil agents from another world were turning the animals against the humans—"

"Hey, I saw that," Clancy said. "Thought it was really something. I enjoyed it."

"The bad guys had this box that would ring out this incredible noise telling the animals when to attack—"

"And you fell in love with the lovely Lovisa Lamore. The Swedish girl, right? She has that cute accent. She's also pretty easy on the eyes, if you don't mind my saying."

"And with her help I was able to prevent the evil agents from taking over the planet."

Rounding the shoulder of one hill, they stepped out from dim shadows. The damp earth brightened. Mountains loomed, and miles of jungle opened beneath them. Momentarily stopping, they breathed in the cooler air and took in the spectacular view.

"Did you see that one, Tyler?"

"*Siren of Jungle Island.*" Tyler responded to the movie star as if confessing some horrible misdeed.

"Didn't you like it?"

"Don't take it personally, Mr. Hunter," Max said. "I think Tyler's just getting a little old for your movies. He'll be seven this year."

"Maybe your next movie should be based on a book?" Lindy suggested.

"I could see Mr. Hunter being very effective as the lead in Dostoyevsky's *The Idiot.*"

Surprised by the viciousness of such humor, Lindy cried out, "Auntie Max!"

"Really, it's okay, dear," Jack said. "Your Auntie Max is just upset with herself for finding me so charming."

Max shook her head, rolling her eyes. As they continued on, their path narrowed, edged by a tall ridge with a steeply cut canyon on one side and open space on the other. Butterflies, some as large as birds, fluttered in the mists.

"Hopefully, your next movie will be something with a lot of food in it," Clancy dreamed aloud. "And we can all be there to share in the feast."

Lindy reached into a growth of large emerald leaves and found an arrow. They each examined it, thinking grimly of its intended target.

"Can I have it?" asked Tyler.

"No. It's very dangerous," answered Max, grabbing the arrow and tossing it aside. "Let's go. We have a lot of ground to cover."

"Hey, look down there!" Tyler exclaimed, pointing into the plunging earth far beneath them. Peering down, they all saw it: through a fine spray clinging to the hillside were the olive-green waters of a beautiful lagoon.

"I didn't realize we were so high," Jack nervously muttered.

"We need to continue heading west."

With the exception of Tyler, they all proceeded, with Max leading. The fruit of a peach palm tree attracted the boy as it angled a short distance off the side of the cliff. He knelt to his knees, stretched an arm out, grasped for the bundle when suddenly the soft soil supporting him shifted and sank.

"Maybe some flyer will see us while we're up high," Lindy said, oblivious to her brother's struggle.

Desperate, Tyler tried scrambling backwards, but beneath him the ground would not stop crumbling.

Looking back, Clancy yelled, "Tyler!"

Max and Lindy whirled. "Tyler!"

Tyler screamed as he slipped off the cliff's edge, falling until—

Clancy snatched the boy's hand and held him tightly, secured by his own weight anchored to the plateau. "Hold on, little fellow! I got you!"

Jack flew into action. "I'll get him!" Racing to the rescue, Jack soon found himself teetering over the precipice, reaching for Tyler but clutching only air. "Uh-oh!" He viciously, frantically wrestled the sky, as the ground beneath him was no longer there— vanished!

"Aaaahh!"

Plummeting into the depths of the lower jungle, shrieking and flailing the entire way, Jack ended his fall with a colossal splash in potentially deadly waters. Indeed, he was alive—but only for the moment! Fate may have played an even more cruel hand than hard-hitting death: flesh-devouring piranha commonly infested the murky bottoms of such lagoons.

Clancy lurched little Tyler up, back onto the narrow path. Together, they dashed to their feet, stunned and horrified by what they saw.

Max and Lindy ran down the hillside, speeding toward the star. In the blink of an eye, Tyler caught up to his aunt and sister. The tubby copilot, yelling, "Mr. Hunter! Mr. Hunter!" fell behind, as downhill running and stumbling for him proved a greater challenge than for the child.

Far below, in the deceptively calm center of all this chaos, Jack rose to the water's surface and spit. Immediately, he recalled the horrifying story of the anthropologist and the poor pathetic pig. Convinced he would soon be lunch for a school of savage fish, he opened his eyes wide, raised his eyebrows, and shook with an uncontainable fear. In an effort to draw as little attention to himself possible, he treaded water with the gentlest of movements, not unlike a falling feather. Up and down his arms waved and legs kicked, noiselessly as possible. "Unbelievable," he whispered between stuttering breaths.

But the quiet did not last! As if from a cannon, little Tyler shot through a wall of trees. "Action Jack!" Flocks of rattled birds launched into the air, chasing others who had already fled the earlier clamor of Jack's fall. Lindy, following her brother, bolted through the same agitated tangle of vines and leaves.

"Tyler! Tyler! Lindy! Wait!" Max, trailing, tried hard to halt both children.

"Mr. Hunter! Mr. Hunter!"

Upon seeing Tyler and Lindy, Jack threw his palms up and kicked more intensely with his feet. "Don't! Stay away from the water!"

With clenched fists thrust forward, Tyler flew into the air, barreling after his hero into the mysterious waters. Lindy, also charging at top speed, caught the shouted warnings from Jack and Max, stopped abruptly at the embankment—teetering back and forth—and then collapsed into the lagoon. Thinking swiftly, she raised the Emily Brontë hardback above her head to keep it from getting soaked.

As Max appeared, ripping through the thicket, she panicked. She covered her face. Her chest heaved. "Tyler? Lindy?"

With water dripping in his eyes and no concern for his safety, Tyler twisted around to his aunt, thinking he might be in trouble. "What?" he innocently questioned.

Red in the face, terribly winded, Clancy finally arrived and asked, "Everybody okay?"

"It's not safe," muttered Max, trembling. However, nothing was happening. She knew the notoriously ferocious eagerness of piranhas, their desperation to instantly devour anything, and yet there were no troubling signs whatsoever.

Jack warily suggested, "Seems to be safe enough. Even kind of nice maybe."

Lindy tossed her book onto the embankment; her glasses and Jack's tuxedo jacket followed. Then she ducked underwater and swam.

Clutching his rapidly pumping heart, Clancy said, "Looks somewhat refreshing." He bent forward, moved both hands to his knees. "Whew! I'm afraid my running days are behind me."

With apprehensions easing, Max sighed, at last relieved. She looked up and ran fingers through her sunlit golden-brown mane and shook it down her back. "Clancy," she then said, patting the panting copilot on the shoulder. "Thanks for catching Tyler."

Clancy straightened, bashfully lifted his eyes to her, mashed his lips together, and said, "Well, it—um—happy to be of assistance!" He crossed his arms, breathed easily, looked out over the lagoon, and locked his stare on a scrumptious vision. "Hey, there's another one of those fruit trees to the side of the water over there." With an added chuckle, he continued, "Maybe this one won't give us so much trouble. I'll—uh—" He tipped the bill of his cap to Max, eyes sparkling with emotion. "I'll see if I can wrangle a few away from the tree for us." Off he hurried, quick-stepping along the rim of the lagoon, feeling forgiven.

Swimming underwater, Jack could not be seen. He aimed for Tyler, maneuvering toward the happy kicking and splashing of small legs and feet near the shallow edge. Facedown, mischievously, Jack moved his shoulders behind the little one's knees and then stood.

Shocked into a fit of screaming laughter, Tyler touched the skies high above the shimmering surface of the lagoon. "Aaah haa!"

With Tyler on his shoulders, Jack playfully pretended to be oblivious. "Anybody see Tyler? I hope he hasn't gotten us into trouble again."

"Aaah!"

Jack scrunched up his face into a mask of confusion and said, "I think there's a bug on my shoulder." With a simple shrug, he tossed Tyler back into the water.

Laughing, they each wallowed in the respite from constant travail. Finding an oasis among the oppressive thickness of the rainforest, their weathered spirits were rejuvenated.

"Is the water warm?" asked Max.

"It's like a bath!" Tyler shouted in return.

"Auntie Max, get in!"

"My clothes will get wet."

"They'll dry," Jack responded.

Max removed her houndstooth jacket and white scarf. She stepped into the water wearing mud-smeared slacks and a white billowy blouse. Once the surface of the water reached her shoulders, a profound expression of relief washed over her.

"Hey, anybody hungry?" Clancy held up melons, one in each hand.

"Throw me one!" said Jack.

Clancy wheeled his arm around and around. "Are you ready?" he asked, rifling one off like a big-league pitcher.

Jack had a knack for slapstick and loved showing off. He raised his hands to catch the flying melon but missed—his forehead caught it instead. He swayed clumsily, rolled his eyes, and fell back into the water.

Clancy, taking a cue from Jack's goofball routine, removed his leather pilot's jacket, leaped into a flip, and slapped down into the lagoon on his back.

The children cackled and cried till it clearly pained them. Little Tyler fell into a coughing fit from swallowing water.

"You're supposed to swim with your mouth closed, idiot."

"Lindy dear," Max scolded. "Don't call your brother an idiot."

"You called Jack an idiot."

"I said he could play *The Idiot*," Max explained defensively. "I was complimenting him."

Jack's smiling face widened in mock outrage. "Oh! I'm not buying that! Do you buy that?" he asked Lindy. Without waiting for a response, he announced, "Auntie Max deserves a splash!"

Tyler and Lindy joined Jack in hurling waves over Max. She screamed in distress and hurried behind Clancy. "Aaah! Clancy, save me!"

Just then something moved in the surrounding forest. Like a ghost, watching, creeping, it appeared and vanished in a flash!

Lindy was the first to spot it. Her arms sank back into the lagoon, and her big blue eyes peered deep into the infinite expanse of green. Without her glasses, she could be sure of nothing.

Alarmed by her niece's sudden gravity, Max turned to the jungle. The playful splashing stopped.

"What?"

"Shh!" Max raised a quick palm to Jack. Worry lined her face. They listened. A gentle swishing of leaves broke above the twitters of parakeets and then stopped.

Jack exclaimed, "I think I just saw something!" but he kept his voice low.

"What did you see?"

"Well … what did you see?"

"I don't know."

"Something's out there," Max said. "Watching us."

The hearts of the stranded raced.

Then strange colorful beings revealed themselves. Only a few appeared at first, then more. Silently, a small all-male population of copper-and-bronze people appeared. The spears held by each were taller than their bodies. Grim faces, full of curiosity and disbelief, simply stared.

Suspicion silenced them all. Uncertainty held for several moments, only to finally be interrupted by the sounds of running feet on the forest floor. Charging from the dark depths of the jungle were small bodies, leaping into the air like frogs chased by fire. They cried out in a clearly diabolical tongue.

Terror-stricken, Jack yelped, "Here they come!"

CHAPTER SIX

The lagoon offensive—as Jack later referred to it—turned out to be a bunch of kids anxious for a swim. They launched themselves into the water, neglecting to notice the white faces watching them. Once the kids came up for air, the shocking sight froze them as it had their elders.

Guarded movements and unspoken questions slowly passed. Finally, Jack nervously said, "There are no women. I'd feel a lot better about this if there were women."

"There must be women," Clancy breathlessly returned. "There are children. This could be a party of hunters and gatherers."

"What are they hunting for?" Jack replied. "That's what I'd like to know."

"Let's just try to relax," said Max.

Several Jivaros who had surrounded the lagoon spoke at last. While doing so, they shook spears in anger and accompanied their words with gestures aimed at the invaders to their land.

"My super-refined instincts inform me they are not telling us to relax and enjoy ourselves—in fact, quite the contrary. If I had to guess, I'd say they want to shake some salt on us and throw us in their soup."

Max hushed Jack with a sharp, "Shh."

Carefully, with eyes ever alert, the stranded five climbed from the water up onto the embankment. Lindy picked up her glasses and put them on. A tribesman grabbed Jack's tuxedo jacket and curiously draped it over his head.

"Everyone stay calm," said Max.

"No problem," Jack muttered without confidence.

Intensely inquisitive, the Jivaros moved closer to those they perceived as oddities, marveling at their clothes and hair. They spoke in harsh, frightening gutturals, and more than one man pointed at them, and then into the depths of the jungle.

Clancy concluded the obvious. "They want us to go with them. Somewhere."

Max drew in a heavy contemplative breath, and said, "So, with them we'll go."

*   *   *

Shafts of sunlight stabbed the forest enclosure. Plants writhed and interlaced with each other in an immense tangle of sky-reaching confusion. Tropical nature struggled upward with ferociousness; however, the movement of such life was so slow that the jungle seemed locked in a state of serene repose.

Adding to the incongruity of this lazy chaotic condition were the indigenous people. Pierced lips, nose sticks, body paint, earplugs, and bird feathers gave the Jivaro people a loudness of character that belied the quiet softness of their footfalls. Their exertions had a graceful, languid rhythm, incapable of being replicated by the westerners who tripped and stumbled over everything.

Laboring through the day's most intense heat, the Jivaros didn't break a sweat. Dear old Clancy, however, suffered terribly—rasping, slapping gnats, and hammering his clumsy feet over the damp earth.

"I did a movie where something like this happened," said Jack, winded. "I think we'll be okay. The important thing to remember is to not engage in any hanky-panky with the chief's daughters."

A native walking behind Lindy poked her with his spear and declared something in an imperious manner. Rumbles of consent passed among the man's clannish cohorts.

"Ouch!" cried Lindy, as the spear hit her. "Stop it!"

Max flew into a rage, running up to and then shoving the surprised warrior. "Hey! How dare you!" she challenged. "She's not some plaything you can toy around with!"

One by one, the entire hunting party stopped, nostrils flared, and a grave silence fell over the whole area. For a moment, the only movements were from the wide eyes of all, anxious to see the reaction from the white woman's outburst.

From the corner of his mouth, Jack muttered, "Max, what are you doing?"

In full voice, Max again went after the same bully warrior, pointing at him. "You keep your filthy hands and sticks off my daughter!"

"Max, stop," Jack snapped before smiling broadly at the warrior. "She's just a little delirious from a lack of raw meat."

"Don't be such a coward, Mr. Hunter! I'm not afraid of these people!"

"I just want us all to get home with the same hat size," Jack responded defensively.

To everyone's amazement, Max grabbed the bully warrior's spear, snatched it from his hands, and broke it over her knee. She threw the broken pieces at the ground and stood defiantly.

Jack swallowed hard, staring down at the spear halves. "Uh …" Turning back to the warrior ingratiatingly, he said, "I'd be happy to buy you a new stick. If you could just point out the direction of the spear store ..."

The grim face of the warrior penetrated Jack's friendly charade. He leaped forward in bare feet, toes splayed. The serpentine designs painted over his sinewy body pressed against Jack, causing a shudder of dizziness.

"Oh dear …" The actor turned timidly from the wild-man stare, the musky smell, the angry visage with its protruding bones and sticks.

"Heh heh heh …"

The suffocating tension abruptly dissipated with one chuckle. Laughter then spread among the Jivaro men. Several pointed at the cracked spear. They punctuated their brutal, angry-sounding talk with gleeful cackles.

Even the bully warrior with the broken spear began to smile.

"Hey," Clancy said. "They're laughing. I think you got them to like us."

Max, maintaining the severity of her hotheaded disposition, took both children by their little hands and moved on with the chuckling parade of warriors. All the jarring jungle noises resumed—the buzzing insects, the looping wails and high-pitched screeches of exotic birds, the chittering of vampires.

Jack hung his lonely head, not moving. While everyone picked up the pace, burrowing again through the unrelenting web of green growth, Jack held back, lost in reflection. She had called him a coward. And she was correct. For the moment, the handsome movie star, the larger-than-life Hollywood hero, hated himself.

A young Jivaro shouted at Jack in their fierce language. "*Eou, shawara nabuh*! *Nabuh*!"

"Don't you think you're being a little hard on me, pal?"

After a second stream of incomprehensible words, Jack said, "Okay. Okay. Put a lid on it, already."

*   *   *

The eerie kingdom of dark shadow and slanted light at last opened to a late afternoon sky where an early moon chalked the blue just above an expanse of distant trees. The large sky revitalized the stranded five, and the vision beneath was astonishingly breathtaking. "Wow, look at the size of that," exclaimed Clancy. After a grueling day, tired heads raised enthusiastically to a majestic and massive community hut.

At one-hundred-fifty feet in diameter, a high round wall of slated palmwood rose and sloped inward, becoming a roof of vines and leaves. Caked with clay, the fortification offered practical protection from the elements and unity among the tribe.

Jack, Max, Clancy, and the kids entered.

A runner must have warned of the white visitors, as the reception was full of intensely curious faces rather than fear or shock. Mostly, women and children came rushing forward, charged with excitement.

The roof extended overhead for several feet in order to shelter hammocks and hearths from rains. The center of the hut was under a canopy of wide-open sky, so that the Indians' domestic life surrounded a central courtyard.

As with the Jivaro men, the women were small in stature and had straight black hair and high cheekbones. Removed from the wilds of the jungle, the indigenous seemed more familiar. Babies cried in mothers' arms. Children chased each other, jumped up and down, and pointed fingers at the strangers. Utilizing wildly exaggerated movements, some returning hunters told of how Max broke a spear. A small sad-faced boy kicked at the dirt while an animated older boy relayed to him his latest adventures.

Max said, "They're going to expect a gift."

"I don't have anything," Jack shrugged.

"Your watch."

Irritated by the suggestion, Jack held up his wrist, boasting, "This is a Curvex Lord. It has seventeen jewels. Cost eighty dollars."

"I'm sure they'll appreciate that."

"It was a gift from Ginny Joy after we shot *She-Devil and the Savage Magi*."

"That sounds very special. Hand it over."

Reluctantly, Jack removed the fancy watch and fastened it to the wrist of the oldest-looking man he could find. "For you," Jack said. "An expression of my heartfelt appreciation and fervent desire to not have my head lopped off and dropped in a vat. Enjoy."

The wrinkly fellow pushed out his chest, proudly putting on view the sparkling treasure. He marched around the enclosure with his arm in the air as if showing off his shiny thing to the sun.

While Tyler and Lindy endured pinches, pulls, and tugs, an intricately decorated man faced Clancy with a gourd. The tubby copilot's nerves stretched; what the heck could this bird want? Clancy asked himself. He hoped for a friendly offering, a welcoming gesture like a fabulous feast with thirst-quenching beverages.

The Indian instead raised the gourd to his own mouth and took a long drink from it. A white liquid that might have been milk poured down the man's chin. He then forcefully spit the white liquid into Clancy's face, sending it out in a fine spray, showering him.

Soaked, the copilot turned to Max seeking an answer to the smelly assault.

"He's complimenting you."

The gourd was lifted to the man's mouth a second time, and from the most serious face Clancy had ever seen came another spell of white rain, spewed as if from a spoiled baby.

"Thank you for that," Clancy said to the man, bowing.

Approaching Max with adoration in his face, a younger man removed a woven fabric from a reed spindle, raising it over Max's head then around her neck. It was a lovely decorative accessory.

"Oh, well—thank you," smiled Max, as flattery flushed her.

Leaping forward, an angry woman lashed out at the smitten man. Surprise turned to hilarity as the man shrunk, terrorized by the cries of jealousy. The explosive scene led to a chase through the hut, and all members of the Jivaro family watched the entertaining fight, cheering and rolling around in hysterics.

It appeared for the moment that the five stranded were relatively safe ...

*   *   *

But as darkness fell, the moon climbed higher and shined brighter. Silver light painted over the surfaces of vines, leaves—and spies! Creeping through the forest, dashing and darting unseen, were warriors from an enemy tribe. Observing the activities of their Ecuadorian rivals with spears, machetes, bows, and arrows in their fists, the hostiles were hesitant, awaiting the attack sign from their Peruvian leader.

This leader was a devilish vision to behold. Eyeballs glistened red. No one dared look into them. A male Medusa, he inspired paralyzing fear—the promise of cruelty on a supernatural level. White buzzard down decorated his black hair. His lips stretched and drooped, packed with tobacco. He stared as if listening to a distant call from unseen realms. Trance-like, he stood taller than most, bedecked in wild flowers, bird feathers, red and black body paint, and the teeth of water monsters around his neck.

His warriors trembled and cowered. His whispers came fast and domineering. On the heels of a few short words, they retreated. When danger bred caution, a wary sorcerer displayed wisdom and gathered loyalty. So they left, with the devil's promise to return.

CHAPTER SEVEN

The night air around the stranded five fluttered with festive noises—laughter, children, and the rhythmic beating of sticks and drums. Lounging comfortably in hammocks along the inside rim of the hut were Jack, Max, and Clancy. Tyler and Lindy played on the hard-beaten dirt floor.

A young Jivaro boy flashed an enchanting smile, grabbed Clancy's cap, put it on his head, and walked away. The much too large cap bobbled atop the little one's head as he skipped around their hammocks.

"Hey, that rascal stole my hat."

"He didn't steal it. He took it," Max explained.

"What's the difference?"

"If he'd wanted to steal it, he'd have waited till you fell asleep."

Clancy rubbed his head, confused.

At the home's center, a roaring fire reached up to sparkling stars. Ghostly shadows sprang from massive flames, dancing behind the wavering orange glow on warm faces. The native boy with Clancy's cap sat on the ground next to Tyler, curious about cards passed back and forth with Lindy.

"Clancy," Max continued. "These people are giving us food and shelter. Consider it a trade."

"But I loved my hat."

"You can get a new hat. The native boy doesn't have that option."

Tyler, overhearing his aunt, handed the native boy some cards. He pointed at himself, saying, "Tyler. That's my name. Can you say it? Tyy-lerrr."

Listening intently, the boy thumbed his chest. "Chohnjo."

"Chohnjo?"

The native boy nodded and Clancy's cap fell over his coal-black eyes. Pushing it back, he looked at the numbers and symbols on his cards, bewildered.

"This is stupid, Tyler. He doesn't even know it's a game." Extending a hand to Chohnjo's fist of cards, Lindy flipped one around so that the face no longer showed. "No," she exclaimed with a finger point.

Tyler set down the remaining cards. As Chohnjo reached for one, Lindy slapped his hand away, startling him.

"Lindy, you're being mean," Tyler argued.

"I am not. I'm educating him."

Tyler sighed, shaking his head. His sister could be this way sometimes. "Let's see what he does, okay? Here," he said, presenting the deck to Chohnjo. "Take a card. Go ahead, take one."

The native boy hesitatingly took a card and scraped the edge of it over dirt, creating a smooth surface. With a fast finger, he drew mysterious designs over the flattened area. Chohnjo punctuated straight lines with dots. Incomprehensible words came quickly, questioningly.

"What's he trying to say?"

Lindy offered her best, well-reasoned guess. "I think he's trying to figure out where we're from."

"We're from Hollywood," Tyler informed the native boy. "And the man in the tuxedo right there is a movie star!" Tyler's voice pitched wild enthusiasm but in return received only a dull stare.

Interrupting them, from the opposite side of the dwelling, a flute added melody to the hypnotic sticks and drums. Rattling a belt of shells, a woman initiated dancing by the fire. Joined by other women, she shuffled and sang, attempting to lift spirits from the Earth.

Knowing festivities were beginning, Chohnjo pulled on Tyler's and Lindy's arms, trying to lead them away. Neither could resist.

"It would appear this native boy would like for us to go with him somewhere, Auntie Max."

"Please, can we go, Auntie Max? Please?"

"Just don't go outside the hut."

"Are you sure it's safe?" Jack questioned.

After watching the children dash off, Max turned a coy smile to Jack. "If anybody tries to pull any funny business, at least we've got me to slap someone around again. Know what I mean, Mr. Hunter? At least we've got me to stand up for us and protect us."

Clancy chuckled. "Ma'am, I believe you could save us from all the evil in the world."

"What do you think, Mr. Hunter? You're the expert."

"Why do you keep calling me Mr. Hunter and not Jack?"

"I like calling you Mr. Hunter. It is your name, isn't it? Or is it one of those phony-baloney names people in Hollywood invent for themselves?"

"Of course, it's my real name," Jack answered defensively. "You'll come around to discovering the real me yet, Miss Daniels."

Communing with spirits continued by way of chanting, singing, and music. The tribal elder with Jack's Curvex Lord moved before the fire. He spoke. His words were sharply chopped and bridged by deep grumbles and roars. Like an old swami carnival barker gesticulating madly, he was captivating and bizarre with his storytelling.

"You know," Jack resumed with Max, "I admit to being a little afraid of all this. But you're afraid too—of a lot of things."

"I'm sure it's just the life you live, Mr. Hunter. My knees would knock too if I was accustomed to calling on servants and stuntmen to handle my dirty work."

Hoping to lower the crossed bayonets of Jack and Max, Clancy tried distracting them from each other. "They sure do laugh and smile a lot, these people."

"For example," Jack whispered to Max, with no regard to Clancy's efforts, "I think you're afraid of your lustful desires for me."

"Oh!" Max bristled. "Really? Mr. Hunter, I can assure you I wouldn't have those kinds of feelings for you if you were the last man on Earth."

"Well, if I was the last man on Earth, I wouldn't care, because the lineup of women would be so long that I would be lusting after a good night's sleep."

"Shh!" She shifted her position, putting a cold shoulder between them.

"They're very physical creatures," Clancy went on with the same intent. "Very affectionate with one another. Fascinating," he exclaimed professorially.

Jack leaned into Max. "Want to know how I can tell?"

"If you don't mind, I'm trying to listen to what the man has to say," Max reasonably stated, referring to the old man's garbled words and animal-trumpeting sounds.

Put off, Jack unleashed a stream of noises mocking the loony speaker.

"Mr. Hunter," cried Max, whirling to him. "I like serious men who do serious things with their lives."

Stabbed again, Jack reflected.

Taking a chance, the film star walked to the center of the hut where the old Indian spoke. He stood hesitatingly before the flabbergasted crowd. Festive melodies and dancing came to a clumsy halt. A white man's participation in Jivaro customs was more than unusual. What could he do? They skeptically wondered.

The actor kneeled to a piece of charred wood, swiped a finger across it, picking up black soot. He touched his face above his lip. Assuming a perfect impersonation, he presented himself to the crowd as Charlie Chaplin.

Jack raised his eyebrows and puckered his mouth beneath a pert moustache, and there he was—the tattered dandy with the absurd duck-waddle walk. Jack pointed a firm finger at the dirt. The elder Jivaro grew curious and looked down. Increasingly animated, Jack pointed again at the unseen thing between them. What could it be? As the old man bent forward to see, so did Jack. Their heads collided, sending each other backward in a shuffling struggle for steady footing.

The Jivaros exploded with laughter.

Infuriated, the old man rushed to Jack, scolded him for his ineptness. Jack dropped his head, offered an apologetic, endearing smile. All seemed fine until the old man turned to walk away, and Jack swiftly kicked him in the backside.

The old man froze—knees bent and arms out, eyes huge, stunned by the insult to his dignity.

From all along the inside rim of the hut came intensifying shrieks of laughter. Despite having never seen a Charlie Chaplin movie, the tribe's beautiful faces burst open and sparkled with tears. Some rolled around in a state of uncontrollable hysterics.

Tyler, Lindy, and Chohnjo were handed a taffy-like food by a female Jivaro; then they rushed toward a better view of the spectacle. "Mmm! Tastes sweet!" Tyler shouted, stuffing his mouth as he settled and watched.

The happy expressions of everyone in the community filled Max's heart with a sensation she had not yet experienced. As Jack's madcap antics went on, she could almost hear the swell of violins. Beside her, Clancy too shook from uncontrollable cackling. Max softened. She was surprised to find herself admitting for the first time that Jack Hunter could be charming. Maybe there was something behind the world's affection for the handsome star after all.

CHAPTER EIGHT

As morning arrived, vivid impressions of joyous dances and exotic rituals from the night before lingered in the cool mist-filled sunlight. Soothing waves of chanting still played in Max's memory. Thoughts moved to her father and herself as a chubby child awaiting his return from faraway adventures. She sighed with a wry smile. The lively damp smell of the jungle returned now that the fire had fallen to ash.

Looking around, Max saw that the hut was mostly empty. Women roasted plantains at their hearths, small children ran around, but the Jivaro men had gone. Having risen early, they started their day as predators, trailing the slumbering beasts of the jungle.

"*Nohi ... Nohi*," Tyler said. With his new friend Chohnjo, who still wore Clancy's much too large cap, Tyler swapped words and knowledge.

"*Matohi*." Chohnjo pointed at his wrist then mimicked the old speaker from the previous night's festivities.

"*Matohi*?" Tyler excitedly repeated. "*Matohi* means wristwatch!"

Lindy lifted her eyes from Emily Brontë and informed her brother, "They don't have wristwatches, dummy. Why would they have a word for them?"

"Oh."

While Jack slept in his hammock, an Indian woman painted a design on his forehead. She and Max exchanged a fast smirk and quiet giggle. She pressed a weave basket against his face and painted through octagonal holes so that the design maintained identical shapes all over his skin.

He awoke. Feeling the woman's hot breath on him, he looked at the six-inch reed pierced horizontally through her nose and three others jutting from her chin. He dropped his eyelids again and said, "You know, when I was dreaming just now, I wasn't in Kukuanaland."

"Do you always sleep so late, Mr. Hunter?"

"It's a talent," Jack answered Max. "And I always exercise my special skills so I don't lose them."

The Indian remained beside Jack holding her weave basket and seed paste for painting. The handsome star looked again upon her bright expression full of perfect teeth, her fast eyes taking in his features.

"I'll have eggs, buttered toast, and coffee." Seeing the thick lumpy seed paste smeared on a fat palm leaf, he went on. "Not interested in goop, thank you. You're quite lovely, and your goop is most generous, but I'd like something from a farm."

"The real men are out hunting for something more appetizing," Max informed him.

"Good. Did someone paint on my head while I was sleeping?"

"We decided it would be nice if you were handsome. And the only thing we could think to do about it was to paint over your face."

"I see. Makes sense. So, how do I look?"

As the Jivaro woman moved off, Max knelt beside Jack's hammock and scrutinized his new face. "I don't think it's enough," she said, her tomboy voice adopting a playful cadence. "Let me see what I can do. Lindy, can I have your purse?"

Lindy brought a petite coin purse to Max. Seeing Jack, the little blonde bookworm mashed her lips together to stifle a smirk.

From the purse, Max produced lipstick. She held Jack's face. "Don't move now," she said with a low voice. She began drawing around his mouth.

"So—"

"Don't talk."

Jack stared into her eyes, not blinking, spellbound by her scent, her touch. Max had never been so near. A rush of dizziness bore into him from the touch of her fingers.

"What … uh … what time does our ship sail for Southern California?"

"Jack, you're supposed to be quiet."

"Oh. Oops."

She continued coloring on him. "I was thinking this morning about all we can learn from these people," Max said. "Survival tips, you know. Toughen ourselves up and then make the trek to the coast better prepared."

"You want to stay here?"

"Would that be disappointing to you?"

"I'm fine where I am."

"You don't miss all your glamorous movie-star friends?"

"I have one friend in Hollywood. Hal Hartford. He was supposed to be directing me again on this picture."

"You're nice. I mean, for someone with one friend. It's a funny contradiction."

"Your hands are soft for someone who tames wild animals for a living."

In a flash, she traded strength for vulnerability. The certainty carried by Max in her every move broke with a subtle lifting of her eyes, a searching stare. "Hold still," she then said. "There's one more thing I want to do."

Jack caught a view of Tyler playing with Chohnjo. Imitating Max, Tyler broke an invisible spear over his knee and threw his arms triumphantly into the air.

Max exchanged lipstick for eyeliner and returned to Jack's face. She used the black pencil to outline a clown smile.

Fully attentive, Jack said, "Careful not to make me look too tough. I don't want the spear carriers to return and think they've been upstaged by some dangerous, highly skilled jungle hooligan."

"All finished." As she said this, her voice suggested something else—something just beginning.

Jack felt her hesitation to back away. Her face remained inches from his. She feigned desire to simply admire her work. But Jack could see her quickened breathing, her roaming eyes anxious to stare into his. "There's nothing more you want to do?"

Max promptly dropped the eyeliner into the coin purse and backed away.

Jack stood. "Well, what do you think, kids? I don't look too scary now, do I?" As laughter assailed him, Jack's eyes remained on Max, whose stare had turned inward. His ridiculous face drew snickers from all around until—

The gate crashed open! Breathless, the tubby copilot stumbled inside.

"Clancy?"

Worry lined his glistening face. He frantically pointed back at the jungle. "Some—some—something's out there! Someone! He's coming!"

"Clancy, what is it?"

Standing stoically at the gate, brawny arms crossed, the Peruvian devil had returned.

Recognition spurred terror in the Ecuadorian tribe. Mothers raced for their children, whisking them into shadows and shouting, "*Pata*! *Shawara*!"

Ugly henchmen crowded their leader with tautly drawn arrows and tightly gripped machetes. Eyes burned with intensity. Striding forward, the invaders flounced to the heart of the defenseless community.

Feisty Chohnjo kicked dirt in the direction of the motley throng. "*Yakúm*!"

"What do we do?" asked Clancy.

"Try to stay calm," answered Max. "Tyler, Lindy, come here!"

The children raced to their aunt and pressed close to her, catching the lightning-quick contagious fear striking them all.

Peculiar attire and pale skin attracted hard stares. The crimson-eyed leader raised a taloned hand and beckoned his forces with an imperious gesture. The man—or demon—was a great mesmerist, silent in his commands. His wicked flatterers watched and obeyed without hesitation, without need of words.

To the stranded five they advanced.

Goons laden with symbols from the darkest arts struck threatening poses, conveying fierce brutality unlike anything thus far witnessed. Perhaps malevolence passed infectiously from the fiendish overstuffed arrogance of their leader, for despite his angered expression, the Peruvian devil gloried in his might. He frightened everyone—even his loyalists—and he gloated with pride in such prowess.

One man lifted a large gourd found among the Ecuadorian's supplies and approached Jack with it. The star did not resist in the slightest as a great heap of water poured down on him, streaking the painted design on his forehead and the lipstick clown smile around his mouth.

"Uh … Max," Jack muttered, as colors streamed down his face. "This would appear to be a serious situation."

Clancy summoned a defiant strength from somewhere deep within. Nearing the blackened remains of the bonfire, he lifted a piece of charred wood.

Not seeing the copilot, Jack continued. "Let's not do anything to further provoke—"

"Jack!" Clancy interrupted. "Let's get 'em!" With this, Clancy hammered a man's head with firewood. The charred wood crumbled upon impact, raising a puff of blackened dust.

The angered warrior with the dirtied hair turned to Clancy who now flashed a stupid grin and held up hands smudged with ash. He snarled through sharpened teeth. Eyes flared like protruding black jewels. A jaguar's fury could not have been more intimidating.

Jack snapped at Clancy. "You could've done more damage hitting him with a teddy bear!"

"I thought—"

The angered warrior unsheathed his machete and thrust it to Clancy's throat.

"Stop!" cried Max, her face purpling with rage.

All eyes turned to the daring woman. Arrows aimed for her, awaiting a simple sign from their leader.

"Uh-oh."

With fists clenched tightly, chin out, and legs braced apart, Max stood still. Her combative glare surprised the enemy warriors.

Jack trembled. A timbre of panic shook in his voice as he said, "Max—remember, they have sharp sticks and—and—and really big steak knives. We have nothing. Just don't—"

"You can stay out of this, Mr. Hunter!"

"For crying out loud, I'm just trying to—"

The Peruvian devil closed the space between himself and Max. Tall for the region, he looked down at her. Up close, the intensity behind the tobacco-sagged face and burning eyes grew even stranger, more frightening.

She blinked. Her pulse quickened.

"Max—"

The mesmerist lifted a hand to his side.

With little delay, he had a bow and arrow suddenly pulled back to launch!

Jack leapt before Max, shielding her. "Hold it!" To the enemy leader, he pleaded, "You don't want to do this! You should know I'm—I'm—I'm surprisingly swift. I don't want to have to hurt you."

The evil one paused, relishing the tension. He then let the arrow fly.

It sunk deep into Jack's thigh. He screamed, "Aaaahh!"

Max covered her horror-stricken, gaping mouth. "Jack!"

"Mr. Hunter!"

Jack fell to the hard-beaten earth and held the arrow with both hands as it pointed skyward, shaking in the steady air.

"Jack—Jack! Are you okay?" Max knelt, placed both hands on the suffering star. "Hang on!"

"Poison? Do they poison these things?"

"I don't know." On her feet again, she raged at the sadistic enemy leader. "That was cowardly! You spineless—" It took a moment to come up with something really good. "Creepo RATS!"

The Peruvian devil gestured toward Max with a mere upturned hand, and with the speed of a hurricane, she was in the air, held high and firmly by a multitude of henchmen. She kicked and writhed, but their grasp was too strong. They carried her away.

"Auntie Max! Noooo!"

Clancy looked on helplessly.

"Put her down! Auntie Max!" Tears welled in the eyes of the children.

Jack mumbled, groaned in agony, drifting from consciousness.

"Mr. Hunter!"

Held over a brawny shoulder, flying toward the gate, Max managed to free a slender arm. "You get your hands off me!" She cried furiously, struggled desperately, and then gripped and unsheathed a machete.

Recognizing their blunder, the warriors dropped Max into the dirt. Instantly, she was on her feet, waving the weapon in every direction.

But she was outmatched. Her attempt was foolhardy.

The enemy leader stretched back his bow, aiming his next arrow at Tyler and Lindy. He was a ruthless vile ogre, and for the first time, he smiled.

Beaten, Max dropped the machete, surrendering.

"Auntie Max!"

Her abductors gathered as a swarm, wrenching her onward, pushing her. For as long as she could, she kept her face to the children—fearing she might never see them again. Scampering off, the enemy tribe was soon gone, disappearing into the infinite expanse of jungle with Max.

The Jivaro women looked on, holding their children tightly, profoundly sympathetic. Incomprehensible words passed softly among them.

Tyler knelt to his hero. "Mr. Hunter, she's gone! They took her!"

"Mr. Hunter, we have to do something!" added Lindy.

Clancy assumed the hard task of taking some parental control. "Easy kids," he comforted. "We have to remove the arrow from the old boy's leg." He pulled on it, tenderly at first, then much harder.

Jack moaned and thrashed in excruciating pain.

"Got it!" Clancy declared, panting with lung-bursting rasps. He tossed the bloody arrow aside.

"We're in big trouble, Mr. Hunter!" Tyler went on.

"We have to go after them," insisted Lindy.

Struggling terribly, Jack managed to squeeze the little girl's hand.

Clancy cradled her in his heavy arms. "No turning yellow on us, angel. It's against the rules, right?"

Jack's breathing stuttered. He shivered, winced.

"Action Jack ..." Tyler pleaded desperately in his ear. "Please get up ... We need you."

With that, Jack's movements ended. His limbs fell, eyes closed. He was gone!

CHAPTER NINE

Though all was blackness, a dazed consciousness of light appeared. Sensations rushed in one direction then another, sickening the star into a state of vertigo.

At some point he realized the light straining for him was not light at all but instead a sound. Faintly, he could hear humming, melodic grumbling. Barely audible at first, it increased in intensity, coiling through the oppressive blackness.

Soft incantations caught him, halted his flailing in oblivion. The voice eventually became clear as a bell, emanating from just above his face. Blackness dissolved to burnt umber then red until—

Jack Hunter's eyes opened.

Framed in clear blue sky, the ancient head of a shaman stared down at him with glazed eyes. Caked in red paste, wrinkled and weathered, the maniacal old witch doctor did not stop chanting. He moved with the throbbing shiver of a possessed wounded animal.

Working swiftly, the shaman swung down to the bloody rip in Jack's tuxedo trousers. He mumbled into the gash as if damaged muscles and tendons could converse.

Long black thorns pierced Jack's leg, surrounding his wound. The star's expression revealed no pain. He rasped longingly from a parched throat. "Max …"

The shaman grabbed palm leaves and rattled them over Jack's body. His rhythmic vocalizing became noisier and more dramatic. For years he had been consuming the ashes of dead ancestors, and now he called upon them, summoning their powers to exorcise demons.

"Jack, how do you feel?"

The words were understood and voice familiar, but Jack knew not who spoke. His head fell to its side. He saw a curious native boy—Tyler's friend—watching closely, expectantly.

The old witch doctor, still humming and grumbling, plucked the thorns from Jack's leg. Once they were removed, the fantastic spectacle of a man threw himself to the dirt. He rolled, clawed, and snarled, battling escaping ghosts. Finally, leaping to his leathery feet, he moved in every direction, dodging madness before fleeing into the vastness of the jungle.

"Mr. Hunter?"

Jack recognized the voice: Lindy! As he began lifting himself, many hands rushed to help. Full awareness of his circumstances returned. Carefully, he stood.

"Jack?"

His reply to Clancy was one of utter befuddlement, a look of complete surprise. He shook his head in disbelief and clasped Clancy's shoulder.

"Are you all right?"

"It's magic," Jack answered. "There's no pain."

"Your leg doesn't hurt at all?"

"No."

Clancy poked a finger against Jack's bloodstained thigh.

"Ouch! Okay, it hurts when you press on it."

Tyler wrapped his arms around Jack's good leg. He looked up at his hero, his face showing too much worry for such a little tyke.

"It's okay, pal. I'm all right," Jack said soothingly.

Warriors had returned from the hunt. A sense of normalcy resumed. Routines of daily life such as roasting plantains, weaving baskets, chopping wood, and nursing babies went on as if nothing had happened.

But Max was out there.

"Auntie Max," muttered Chohnjo, observing Jack's distant stare.

Tyler nodded. "Auntie Max."

Clancy shuffled around awkwardly, kicked at the dirt, and jammed his hands in his pockets. "Makes our return to civilization a bit more urgent, I suppose. Proper authorities probably have some sway with these people. The boy's been picking up some words. Maybe with a little effort, these people could direct us to someone who could help."

"We have to find her," Tyler insisted.

"I suppose," Jack said, answering Clancy's sensible analysis.

"Action Jack …"

"There's nothing we can do by ourselves, Jack."

The hearts of the children were further crushed by Clancy's gently put words. Their faces lowered. Clearly, they had been hoping for something else.

The Hollywood star limped forward until he could peer into the grim forest. "She's out there. Somewhere."

"We don't know where," Clancy reminded him. "And if we did—well, how would we take on an entire tribe?"

Tyler pointed at his friend. "Chohnjo knows where they are."

"They have machetes, Jack. Bows and arrows. Who knows what else? We would be crazy to think—"

"Yeah. I know."

Devastated, Tyler dragged his feet to a hammock, sulking. His sister's shoulders slumped. She seemed unable to move, frozen by grief.

Jack watched the children for a moment and then again cast his gaze into the dark jungle. He pushed his square jaw forward and took a long pensive breath. Insects wailed like warning sirens.

The mad cries of monkeys bullied him. Jack considered the bloodsucking gnats, hunger, vampires, ghosts, dinosaur snakes, and water monsters—the horrid gauntlet they might traverse before even the worst of dangers.

"Mr. Hunter … Jack? What are you—uh—"

"What are we if we have no courage, Clancy?"

The tubby copilot removed his mitts from his pockets, shifting nervously. He then took deep breaths and rubbed his potato head having a pretty good idea where this was going.

Jack whirled to the kids. "Tyler!"

Lindy's eyes lifted. Her brother remained buried in his little arms.

"My friends," Jack asserted, "what are we if we have no courage? We face an impossible situation here. Some might call me crazy for considering this. But, well, if following my heart makes me crazy, then so be it."

Tyler's eyes eagerly popped open.

Jack winked at the boy. "What do you say we rescue the beautiful princess from the dreaded chest pounders of doom?"

"Yes!" Beaming suddenly, Tyler shot from the hammock like a cannonball, wide-eyed and racing to Jack. He cried, "You can count on me, my friend!"

"Me too!" added Lindy, hopping up and down with excitement.

"Well, guess I'm in as well," mumbled Clancy with a fretful chuckle. "All for one and one for all!"

*   *   *

Jack, Clancy, Tyler, and Lindy followed Chohnjo's lead, running, ducking, and slapping away fat leaves. The star supported his weakened leg with a walking stick, hobbling along, trying bravely to maintain a swift pace.

Carved by great clumps of growth and rushing streams, the jumbled earth presented a maddening challenge to the westerners. Trekking through the jungle had been tough when they weren't chasing someone; now, it seemed they dared the impossible.

The native boy, however, flitted through the forest neither perspiring nor gasping for breath. He moved with the sure-footed spring of a cat through the thicket.

"Chohnjo!" Tyler called, as he noticed Jack falling behind. "Rest."

Slowing to a stop, Clancy gripped his chest, struggling for soggy air. Jack leaned against a tree and wiped his forehead with his grubby white shirt. Chohnjo wrinkled his face in wonderment as he watched Lindy and Tyler plop down, winded as well.

"Um…" The copilot raised a finger, drawing attention. "While resting a moment, I'd like to ask … I don't mean to be a dark cloud here, but what are we going to do when we find Miss Daniels? And please don't give me any of these movie-hero lines like, 'With the sun at my back and the wind in my sails.' That's all hogwash. I'd like specifics."

Jack stared blankly. "I don't know," he reluctantly admitted.

Lindy said, "We could sneak in during the night or something."

Tyler suddenly brightened with inspiration. "*Doctor Rogue and the Snare of the South Seas!*"

"Wait a minute," Clancy exclaimed, his wheels spinning. "I saw that picture."

"Remember the part—"

"With the vines. That's a great idea. There's fishing line in the supply bag, which might work even better."

Lost, the handsome star asked, "Can someone fill me in on what happened?"

"You don't remember?"

"But wait," Clancy said, now shaking his head dismissively. "It won't work. We don't have any of the lightning-bolt potion he used as distraction."

"Oh. I remember."

"You and Jack could stage a fight," Tyler suggested.

Clancy straightened. "I suppose that might work." He excitedly rubbed his fat hands together. "Of course, it would be a privilege to do a fight scene with Jack Hunter! But is it easy?" he asked the actor. "I've never done it."

Jack perked up, elated by the chance to utilize his unique skills. He raised his fists. "Sure. That is, it's easy for those of us who know what it is we're doing. The trick is to only throw a punch with your back to your audience. That way you can miss by three feet, but if your opponent reacts at the right time, it looks real. Allow me to demonstrate."

Lining himself up with the kids at his back and Clancy before him, the movie hero asked, "Are you ready?"

"I think so."

Jack swung wide. He launched a haymaker, which unexpectedly clobbered poor Clancy, knocking him hard to the ground!

"Ooh! My gosh, I'm so sorry!"

"Clancy, are you okay?" Lindy knelt over the copilot examining his red face and rapidly blinking eyes. "Clancy?"

"I'm all right—I think."

"Sorry about that, old pal."

Clancy got to his feet, rubbing his cheek.

"Misjudged the space between us," Jack continued apologetically.

"Quite all right. Accidents happen."

"Let's try again."

"Any more practice swings, and we might be defeated before we arrive," cautioned Lindy.

"The kid makes a good point there, Jack."

"We should move on," the girl advised.

Quickly, Clancy supported her judgment. "That gets my vote."

"The truth is," Jack said, "Stuntmen have always handled fight scenes for me."

"Makes sense. We'll save my old noggin for the real show, shall we?"

Off Tyler's nod, Chohnjo dashed again, burrowing through a slim trail fringed with bushes, branches and the never-ending possibility of brutal savagery. Clancy shook stars from his head and soldiered on as Jack limped behind, mumbling, "I could have been a stuntman, if I wasn't so good looking. A smart person follows where their strengths lead."

*　　*　　*

As the long and anxious day neared its end, the moon's silver light painted over vines, leaves, and the peering faces of Jack, Clancy, and the kids. They crept through the forest, dashing and darting unseen until there appeared before them the colossal exterior of the Peruvians' circular fortress.

Looking upward, on edge in enemy territory, Jack asked, "Sure we have the right address?"

"It's a good bet we do," whispered Clancy. "Take a look at those skulls, scattered and stacked along the walls. Probably there to frighten off strangers."

"Unless they're cannibals and the trash collector's on strike."

"I prefer to assume that's not the case."

"Makes two of us."

Great fire-lit plumes of smoke billowed from the center. Drums pounded aggressively, as did Jack's heart. Desperately worried, he relied on the calm face of Chohnjo to assure him no harm would come to Max overnight. The little guy was certain of their mission and would not have guided them for nothing, Jack reasoned.

Still, they mulled over the myriad of ghoulish rituals Max might meet. "I really hope this hair-brained scheme of ours works," Jack said quietly.

"We should go," Lindy warned. "When clouds cover the moonlight, we're not going to be able to see anything. It'll be too dark to walk, and we want some distance between us and them so we can build a fire."

"That's what I call using your noodle, kid," Clancy offered as compliment, punctuating it with a pat on her shoulder. "Good job."

Sometime later, their own fire burned. While the others slept, Jack remained awake. He stared through the high canopy of trees listening to Clancy's snores, along with the more perilous rumblings of the forest. The wilder sounds seemed to reach a cacophony at night. Jack sighed over the unrelenting dangers they faced and turned his head to Tyler and saw that he too was awake. The boy rested wide eyed, lying stretched out on his back, arms folded beneath his head—perfectly imitating Jack. The star turned back to the sky and smiled.

Dark clouds now blanketed the space above the trees. However, a bright hole punctured the blackness. Jack held his gaze within that sparkling space, reflecting on his strange fate and the bejeweled wonder of the heavens.

CHAPTER TEN

The next day, inspired by the brilliant minds behind *Doctor Rogue*, devious traps were set throughout the jungle. Jack, Clancy, and the kids spent the morning tying fishing line between trees, just above the forest floor. They marked the trees appropriately so they could later relocate which paths had been set for trickery.

Alone, securing a line at the bottom of one of these forest giants, Jack was unexpectedly tapped on the shoulder from behind. "Tyler?" he breathed voicelessly, eyes rolling aside. "Ty—Ty—Tyler?" Tapped a second time, he whirled, jumping at the sight.

A monkey's mouth widened and giggled.

Jack calmed, relieved he hadn't been discovered by a machete-wielding maniac. "That's funny to you?" he whispered.

It was a white-faced capuchin. The mischievous goof laughed even louder at Jack's embarrassment and dropped into a series of flip-flops and somersaults.

"You have a sick sense of humor, buster! Now go on! Get out of here!"

In a flash, the capuchin skipped off, cackling as he went.

"Stupid monkey. Running around scaring everyone, thinking its funny."

A short time later, Jack reconnected with Clancy. They were set, ready to go. With the kids safely some distance back, the copilot and film star crept to the edge of the forest where the noon sun broiled. The hut's high gate was cracked, and movement inside was somewhat visible.

"You see her?" Jack asked, narrowing his eyes through tall grass.

"No."

"That little Chohnjo better be right about this. How many lines did we set?"

"I don't know. A couple dozen or so."

"Well … I guess this is it. Ready?"

"Are you?"

"Yeah."

"Okay. I'm ready too. Are you ready?"

"Am I ready? We've been through this already. I'm ready! I'm ready! Are you ready?"

Clancy steeled himself. "I'm ready."

They each swallowed hard, nervous, took deep breaths, and marched into the open.

"Wait, wait, wait!" Clancy quickly muttered.

"Clancy, we're at the doorstep. There's no going back now."

"I'm just—I'm still a little unclear about the fighting part."

"Just follow my lead and make sure when you lose your temper and get angry at me that it looks real. I know acting's not your game—just do the best you can. We'll be fine."

Jack and Clancy shook hands and gave each other a good pat on the shoulder. Still using a staff to support his leg, Jack stepped to the tall palmwood gate and knocked. While waiting, Clancy nervously whistled a happy tune, fighting his fears.

A scarlet macaw trumpeted a warning overhead. Nothing else moved or made a sound.

"Maybe they don't know what a knock on the door means."

Jack swung open the gate. "Anybody home?"

Rising and hissing in their guttural tongue, Indians quickly charged, waves of them rushing forward. A horde of gruesome bodies, fully painted in seed paste, set arrows, raised clubs, and shook spears.

Beneath a distant overhang was Max, tied with vines to a stake and gagged with a piece of torn blouse. The Indians had extravagantly accessorized her in shells, flowers, bones, and teeth. She appeared unhurt and as feisty as ever.

The handsome star made a dramatic show of lowering his long staff to the ground and leaving it. "We come in peace!" Jack announced, winking at Max. He could see her pull on her restraints with escalating excitement.

His words triggered agitation, aggression, and confusion. The Indians fluttered around with wide eyes full of distrust. A man with a monkey skull in his headdress spit a tobacco wad in his hand and fast-balled it at Clancy, smacking him in the gut.

"Thank you, good sir," Clancy said, smiling. He then shifted the direction of his words toward Jack, speaking low from the corner of his mouth. "Where's the tall fellow who got you with the arrow?"

"I was asking myself the same thing." Jack flashed a smile and addressed the tribe. "Friends! Have I got a bargain for you!"

A warrior taunted Jack with an eerily accurate jaguar roar.

"Now wait! Just give us a minute! You guys are gonna love this! You see, we came here in an airplane!" Using exaggerated gestures to communicate, Jack swooped around with arms extended, vocalizing an airplane sound. "This airplane," he continued. "Happens to be filled with weapons!"

Spear-carriers pounded the dirt. Other natives shook bundles of shells matching their rhythm. "*Púju! Púju! Púju!*" they cried threateningly.

For the rescuers, nerves went from nail biting to near panic. "We've got some of the big knives you like, whole bags of them!" Jack pointed at their machetes, his voice rising. "And we've got bows and arrows! Guns!"

"They seem to be loaded up with weapons already, Jack. Maybe we should tell them we have something else."

Sticking to the plan, Jack continued. "So anyway, folks, if my friend here doesn't object, I'm happy to give you the whole shebang!" On cue, Jack turned to Clancy expectantly, but Clancy did nothing.

"Uh …" Jack went on, unsure. "I'll give you all the killing things we've got! That's what I'll do! Yessiree, if you're a hostile people looking for a deal, then this is your day!"

Jack turned eagerly, desperately, to Clancy. "I hope I'm not upsetting you, making you angry, giving away our weapons like this?"

Baffled, Clancy scratched his old noggin. He knew he had a role to play but couldn't remember what. He thought hard.

Meanwhile, the circle of villains closed in!

"Uh …" Jack went on with increasing urgency. "What else? A bazooka! A cannon! But my friend here would probably get very mad if I gave you the cannon! Right, friend?"

"What cannon?"

Jack turned to Clancy, grabbed him by the collar, and cried, "I'll give them the cannon if it pleases me!" He pushed Clancy and swung wide with his fist, launching a deadly haymaker. It was an impressive-looking blow; however, it missed Clancy by at least seven feet.

Seizing the moment now, and convinced of the fight-scene illusions Jack had educated him on, Clancy pretended to take the punch. He fell back and rattled his head, shaking out stars. "Ooh, I'll get you for that!" challenged Clancy, now playing along in a feigned angry voice. He shuffled swiftly on his feet, guarding himself with elevated knuckles like a boxer.

The stunning display of mettle and backbone they had planned turned into something more closely resembling absurd theater. Nevertheless, they carried on, managing to mesmerize— and entertain—their enemy.

Sneaking inside the gate, unseen, hurried Lindy and Tyler. They watched Clancy take a wild swing at Jack, miss by a mile, and still miraculously knock Jack to the dirt.

Even with restricted movements, Max could be seen rolling her eyes and shaking her head.

"Its amazing Mr. Hunter's life hasn't been more of a mess," Lindy said, articulating what her aunt could not. After stopping her brother from crossing the courtyard to Max, she pointed to Indians surrounding the captive.

Spitting out a mouthful of dirt, Jack also noticed he had failed to lure all the natives from Max. He got to his feet and gave an apologetic look to Clancy. "Sorry about this, old boy," he mumbled, before lurching forward and walloping the dickens out of the poor old copilot for real.

Clancy went down hard, stunned. He shook his head and pointed a shaking finger at Jack from the ground. "That's twice you've given me a knuckle sandwich! What the heck kind of actor are you?"

"I'm trying to get all the hooligans away from Max!"

"Oh, I see." He stood and smacked off dirt from the back of his coveralls. "Well, let's see if this does it!" Clancy pummeled Jack's face with an uppercut.

The actor staggered back, holding his bloodied nose. "You punched me!"

"And what of it?"

"Do you know how much this face is worth?"

Clancy bounded forward and decked him again. With Jack on the ground, Clancy thrust his triumphant fists in the air, jumping around to the wild cries of the natives.

"Fine," Jack said. "If that's the way you wanna play it." Jack painfully stood, dusting himself off. He lunged at Clancy, leading with his shoulder and gripping his wounded thigh, and slammed into the tubby copilot's belly.

Laughter spread among the natives. The dense air filled with noises, rising emotions. Some imitated the fight, wrestling ghostly opponents, thrusting and slashing with fists and weapons. As an audience, they all now began to close in around the melee.

Tyler and Lindy dashed to Max. "Are you okay?" Lindy whispered as they reached her. Both children grappled with knotted vines.

Unable to loosen anything, Tyler shouted, "I can't untie it!" In a fit of frustration, he used his little teeth, biting at Max's bindings.

"Shh!" Lindy scolded him and then—struck by an idea—removed a necklace of sharp animal teeth from Max. She used a long jagged tooth to saw the vines.

"Hurry!"

"Shut up! I'm going as fast as I can!"

Max reprimanded both, but the tight gag around her mouth suffocated her words.

A vine snapped! "Got it!" Together they unraveled what had been wrapped around her entire body.

"C'mon!"

Free from the stake, Max pitched forward and dropped like a cut piece of timber. A dirt cloud filled the air following the impact. Additional vines remained around her hands and feet.

From a distance, Jack caught sight of the children's efforts. He pushed Clancy back and grabbed his staff from the ground. "We're shifting our strategy!" He swung the staff at an Indian, smashing the man's face, launching broken piercings into the sky and putting a decisive end to the tribe's entertainment.

Bloodthirsty cries clamored. Bowstrings stretched and spears raised.

Jack grabbed the neck of a woman, pulled her before him, using her as a human shield. "Sorry," he said to her. "I'm usually much better than this with the ladies."

Clancy clocked an Indian with a fast combination of punches. He then ducked from an arrow soaring above his scalp. With an eye on Jack, he grabbed a young man from behind, pulling on a necklace of sharp teeth and choking the youngster into playing shield for him.

As Jack and Clancy raced to Max and the kids, struggling with their captives, Lindy pulled a palm frond tray from beneath a fruit display. She raised it as a shield, huddling behind it with Tyler as they crouched before their aunt.

Arrows thumped into the wall behind them. With every passing second, the predicament became more disastrous. Chances of escape dwindled.

"We have to make it to the open gate!" Jack cried as he reached them. He pushed the native woman aside and lifted Max, tossing her over his shoulder.

Clancy tightened his grip on the youngster's choke collar and stood before them all with his legs braced, his pained jaw tightened. "Ready Jack?"

"Ready as I'll ever be! Let's go!" But as soon as they began, they stopped. Their hearts sunk.

Framed by the open gate, the Peruvian devil suddenly stood waiting! He greeted his visitors with a sharp-toothed grin of death and hate, a cocksure glare welcoming them to his evil lair. Flanking him were his henchmen—lips bulging from tobacco, bodies painted in serpentine and circular designs, mindlessly obedient to demands no matter how deranged.

All eyes turned to Jack. What to do now?

"I'm thinking!"

Max, gagged, hanging over the star's broad shoulder, mumbled something that sounded like sarcasm.

An arrow crossed the courtyard, its tip drenched in flames. It struck Lindy's tray, setting it on fire. She screamed.

"Give it to me!" shouted Jack.

"It's on fire!"

Jack snatched it and threw it at the back wall. The woven vines and palm fronds ignited into a shocking blaze. As the inferno rushed upward and the Indians leapt into a wild frenzy, Jack commanded his friends. "Follow me!" He led them, charging straight through the wall of flames.

CHAPTER ELEVEN

The Indians thunderously trampled their land. They hurled spears, shot great bursts of arrows, and blew poison darts.

Max's daring rescuers fled at a disadvantage; the Peruvian tribe knew every green inch of their surroundings. However, despite the continued danger nipping at their heels, Jack and his friends were elated by their own audacity. The rash exploit had been accomplished. Though perhaps not with the swashbuckling heroism imagined, the scheme still worked.

"Jump!"

As they now plunged triumphantly, though still desperately, through the jungle, Clancy took up the rear, beating on his smoking britches.

"Jump!"

Chohnjo's face, beaming with excitement, popped out from behind a bush. He pointed at the mark on another tree.

"Jump!"

Max groaned over Jack's shoulder. Carried like a sack of grain, humiliated, she now had to stomach the leaps and landings, bounding this way and that.

"Jump!"

Chohnjo joined in their bold escape, skipping over multiple wrappings of fishing line stretched between trees.

In savage pursuit, the Indians' bone-chilling cries shook the forest. Their volley of weapons couldn't penetrate deeply into the thicket, which infuriated them all the more. As one brute suddenly tripped, all those behind toppled over him.

Catching up to his forces with eyes burning red, the evil leader stepped over his bumbling henchmen. He glared, cast fast spells into the dim darkness beyond, and pulled a papyrus plant from the soft ground. A small gourd hung among his accoutrements. He spit into it and swirled the papyrus into the gourd.

With his followers returning to their feet and removing tobacco from their mouths, the Peruvian devil painted their jagged teeth snow white.

They then yapped and howled like fiendish jackals. Bellies tightened with rage. Necks corded and faces purpled. They cried out curses, jumped in place and thumped spears into the earth, drumming for the path to black magic. Finally, bristling with all the wicked energies they could summon, they charged forward again—

And tripped!

After piling on top of each other a second time, they became convinced a malevolent shaman had bewitched them with voodoo. Shaking, mumbling in fear, they retreated, scrambling in all directions—defeated.

Foiled, the Peruvian devil's rage reversed. He seethed at his own. To the fates he cursed and shot a poison arrow at the sun. With no choice, he walked back to his burning home, his foul heart still thirsting for blood.

*　　　*　　　*

"Most women would appreciate being rescued from headhunters," Jack grumbled as Max—still bouncing over his shoulder—squirmed and protested.

Exhausted, they stopped running. Listening carefully to their surroundings and hearing nothing, they felt secure that if they took a quick moment to catch their breath, no harm would result. And so they did.

Wincing from his wound, Jack put Max down. He worked at the vines around her ankles. "Maybe if we leave you gagged, you and I might get along better."

"Shh!" Lindy hissed, admonishing Jack. "I hear something."

"What?"

"Someone's coming."

All at once, they silenced their breathing, concentrating on any sound beyond the normal hoots and howls, twitters and squawks.

Quiet moments passed. Max jumped to her feet, still gagged. Jack began untying the vines around her wrists. "I don't hear anything," he whispered. After loosening the bindings to Max's hands, Jack's head shot up, alert to the snap of a twig and rustle of leaves.

They all heard it!

Leaping from an embankment and striding toward them, a massive jaguar appeared. Baring deadly fangs, he unleashed a throaty snarl, loud enough to shake grubworms from the trees. The ill-tempered beast seemed like he hadn't had lunch in a thousand years.

Eyes widened. Frightened hearts throbbed. Max struggled with her gag while Jack asked her, "Isn't this your area of expertise? Can't you get him to roll over and lick himself silly or something?"

Lindy answered for her aunt. "It takes months to properly train a wild animal!"

As the jaguar lurched, Jack responded with a hearty roar of his own and a broad swing of his staff. He waved the stick in the cat's face, taunting it, luring it from the others. "That's it. Come on, sweetheart."

"Jack, be careful," warned Clancy.

"Take Max and the kids and run. Go!" the handsome star demanded. "You guys get out of here."

"We're not leaving you, Jack."

Terribly frustrated, Max couldn't untie the knot in her gag.

"Go. I'll catch up."

"Mr. Hunter," said Lindy, sounding very determined. "We're staying right here with you, and that's that."

Stepping backward, Jack tripped. He fell. The jaguar dived over him, sunk his dripping jaws into Jack's staff. They each wrestled for it as—

Tyler breathlessly covered his face. "Action Jack. No!"

The beast ripped the staff away, tossing it. Looming above Jack now like a powerful prehistoric monster, he unexpectedly hesitated. Yellow eyes peered into the muted depths of the forest, searching.

"Uh …"

Though much smaller than the first, a second jaguar appeared!

"Another one!" cried Clancy.

"It's a cub," Lindy explained.

A deep rumble emanated from the protective parent. Several tense-filled seconds passed before the large one chased the little one off. Together they bounded through trees, disappearing in a flash.

Jack's head dropped back, eyes remaining open and unblinking. He lay motionless among moss and bugs breathing in the broiling humidity. He smiled finally.

Leaves rustled once more. A twig snapped.

"Shh!"

Backs stiffened yet again. Hearts raced as before—until a native woman ran forward, scooping Chohnjo up in her arms. She scolded and squeezed him, lovingly.

Becoming visible all around, emerging from the shadows, were the Ecuadorian tribe. A more welcome sight could not have been imagined. For despite their coarse black hair, reed-pricked chins, earplugs, and unusual fragrance, their faces were friendly. In them the stranded five's trust had been well placed.

One of the men easily snipped Max's gag free using the tip of his machete.

"Aaahh!" she breathed. "Thank you so much!" Max then bundled Tyler and Lindy in her arms, holding them tightly.

Clancy joined Jack on the ground, allowing relief to flood through his system. He offered his hand to shake as congratulations on their victory. "Are you hurt?"

"I'm fine," Jack said, shaking his hand. "How about yourself, old boy?"

"I feel great."

Lindy and Tyler stepped before Clancy and Jack, their faces set to express something of great magnitude. Clearing her throat and straightening her glasses, Lindy spoke first. "Thank you, Mr. Hunter. Thank you, Mr. Clancy." Very formally, she shook each of their hands.

"This has been but one of many adventures together," Tyler said, with the dramatic lilt of a movie hero. "But what makes this one so special is that this time you saved my Auntie Max. You are a man of great courage, Dr. Rogue. And you as well, his faithful copilot."

As Tyler extended his hand, Jack pulled him into a hug. From the corner of his eye, Jack thought he saw Max watching at a distance, longing for the same affection.

*　　　*　　　*

With the onset of twilight's dim sparkle, sunrays fallen and vanished, the travelers relied on flaming torches to light their way.

The tribe remained cheerful, talkative, at ease in the enclosed liveliness of endless jungle.

Max said little as they walked.

Jack caught her glancing at him from time to time, sensing that her thoughts had something to do with him—but what exactly those thoughts were, he did not know.

"Seems we've walked over half the Earth," said Clancy.

"If you walk long enough, you can fall into a time travel vortex," Tyler explained. "Maybe we'll find dinosaurs."

Lindy turned to her brother with a mocking expression. "Or maybe we'll time travel far into the future when you're not so stupid."

The front of the procession suddenly became more spirited. Very quickly, all the Indians were chattering over one another. Some ran forward, impatiently tearing through the darkness.

Beyond the flickering torches, between the blackened tangles of trees, a lively glow beckoned. Billowing smoke lifted the light, rushing it upward to the stars.

"This can't be their home," said Max. "We haven't traveled far enough."

As they edged closer to an immense clearing, Jack said, "Well, we've certainly arrived somewhere."

"Yes. Somewhere less primitive."

CHAPTER TWELVE

After all they had been through, the stranded five found it difficult to express the tremendous rush of optimism they felt in assessing this latest encampment. Among nighttime feasts, fires, and dancing, a crowd of bustling revelers included a handful of natives in white T-shirts. As well, surrounding two huge circular huts were a series of smaller homes made of palmwood and clay, square in shape.

A monkey scuttled up to Jack, pointing to the star between flip-flops in the dirt. Jack's immediate reaction was to ignore the little guy, recognizing him as the same white-faced capuchin from earlier in the day.

Max, sensing Jack's awkwardness, asked, "A long-lost relative?"

"I scared the dickens out of this goof earlier today. Must've followed us here."

As they walked, the little knuckle dragger shuffled alongside Jack, mimicking perfectly the bedraggled star's limp. Wanted or not, the spirited monkey remained, adopting Jack as his new best friend.

The tribe who called this place home greeted the Ecuadorian Indians warmly, as friendly neighbors. Some natives exchanged gifts and ceremoniously showered each other with white spit.

"They're familiar with westerners," Max said, picking up only subtle looks of curiosity. Her voice was careful not to insinuate too much hope that someone here might help them return to civilization.

Preoccupied with danger, Jack remained pensive. "I still can't escape the feeling that they're looking at my head and thinking it needs to be smaller."

"They'd be correct in that assessment."

Following along, stepping inside one of the circular huts, Clancy hoisted his nose into the air and breathed deeply. "Lovely smell. Some kind of roast. I'm starving."

Seeing more white T-shirts, Max said, "This might be a better place for us to stay. Looks like they may have had visits from missionaries or malaria-control people. If that's the case, it's entirely conceivable they'll be back." Her eyes remained wary, scrutinizing, and protective of her companions. She supplemented her thoughts with a sigh. "But, will they return in two weeks or two years? That's the question."

Spoken in the glow of starlight and fire, those words meant little to Jack. He forced his stare away from Max's gorgeousness, her slender figure etched in silver and gold, catching sight of an Indian bedecked in toucan feathers and buzzard down—carrying a shotgun. The man simply passed without acknowledgement.

"Maybe we should sleep in shifts so that one of us always has an eye open," Jack suggested.

"You feel like sleeping?" Max huffed.

"I haven't slept in two days. Clancy and I went a few rounds of championship boxing. I got shot with a bow and arrow—like I'm a deer or something. Then I was magically healed by a loony witchdoctor's hocus-pocus. So, yes, pajamas and sleep right now would be terrific. I'm tired."

From blackened shadows, a voice called. "How you like cup of coffee?"

"Who said that?"

Like a ghost assuming flesh, a bearded face materialized. "Over here." With a single step forward, the man allowed firelight to warm his weathered features. Eyes were sparkling black jewels, questioning in their gaze. "I am Umberto Alléjandro Quinto."

Max noticed wood boxes and potato sacks around the man's heavy boots. She smiled but did so reservedly, mirroring his suspicions. "Maxine Daniels. The children are Tyler and Lindy. The Jivaro boy's name is Chohnjo."

The dark man nodded silently to each of them.

"Clancy," the copilot said, identifying himself. He moved to tip his cap then caught sight of it still on Chohnjo's head.

"Jack Hunter," the star stated, expecting some recognition but receiving nothing.

"You're a trader?" inquired Max.

"A trader. *Sí.*"

"Are you here with anyone else?"

"I work alone."

With swagger in their step, Indians approached. They spoke harshly, pointing at the merchandise.

The trader kicked a potato sack, producing a clattering of metal sound. He spoke in their language, adding an aggressive gesture implying offense taken. Manly tempers flared before the trader pulled back, calmed. Squeezing his beard with a rough hand, contemplative, he bit his lip, watching the Indians storm off.

Red embers glowed beneath a nearby steaming kettle. The trader lumbered to the kettle and poured coffee into small bowls.

Max pressed the man further. "Are we near a town or village?"

"You do not find dis place to be of suitable comfort?"

"We're lost. Maybe you can help us—"

"We're supposed to be on a movie set," Jack interjected.

"Movies? I seen de movies—at a place in Colombia." The man pulled a polite grin, which didn't reach his eyes as he served coffee.

"Thank you. You're very kind." Max sipped the coffee. "Mmm, delicious," she said. "Look, mister—*señor*—" Max tilted her head, offering her warmest, most irresistible face. "We need to find a way back to the United States, to California."

"Hollywood," Jack clarified.

Umberto Allejandro Quinto stared hard at Lindy, watching her clutch her book with both hands, sensing her devotion to it. "Little one wit' de glasses—let me tell you, a Bible is not goin' to protect you very well in de Amazon."

"It's Emily Brontë," explained Lindy.

The man scrunched his lined face into a tight knot, scratched his ragged head, and said, "You are not from de churches up north?"

"No," Max cut in. "We're not missionaries."

The trader pulled his shoulders back. "Aah!" he said, relaxing his guarded posture, suddenly bursting with geniality. "Das good! 'Cause I seen bad tings happen to dos peoples. Some of dem very nice, an' still bad tings happen. Dis place, very dangerous to stay. I seen—"

Umberto Allejandro Quinto abruptly shook his head, rattled his memories and settled dark eyes on Jack. "*Uno momento!*"

Alarmed, Jack braced himself.

"Jack Hunter? *The* Jack Hunter? Saturday-matinee hero Jack Hunter?" He threw his arms wide and beamed. "De one who sleeps wit all de women!"

"What?"

"I am a big fan!"

"Sleeps with women?"

Slicing through Jack's embarrassment with unrestrained feistiness, Max said to the trader, "So, do you think you'll be able to help us?"

"Jack Hunter!" he continued incredulously. "De Action Jack! Oh, of course! It would be my great pleasure to help Jack Hunter an' amigos!"

"Great."

"I could be like Pepe in dat movie wit you … What was de title?"

"Oh … *Daredevils of Mercy and the* … Wait. No … *Boneless Death of the* … Uh … *Boneless Daredevil* …?"

"Yes! Dat was it! What an excitement, eh?"

"One of my favorites."

Max shoved Jack aside. "*Señor* Quinto—"

"Call me Pepe."

"Pepe. Your help would be terrific. We would be so grateful."

"Sure. No trouble."

"May I ask how exactly you would be able to assist us? Is there a way you could contact someone? Is there a boat?"

"I have Staggerwing."

"Ha!" Clancy jumped. His fingers fidgeted with the air, and his feet danced. "Oh, boy!" he exclaimed. "A Staggerwing is a beautiful plane, Jack! And powerful! It could get us home without a hitch for sure!"

The stranded five gawked at the Latino as if from divine hands he had been sent. Even the monkey bounced and laughed, emulating the soaring spirits of his new friends.

"Tomorrow," Umberto Allejandro Quinto stated. "We fly Staggerwing to California."

"Tomorrow?"

Max cried, "Tomorrow! Oh, that's fantastic!" She wrapped her arms around Tyler and Lindy, squeezing them till their joy turned to playful protests.

"Tomorrow?" Jack repeated. "That's—that's—that's real soon!"

"It's a miracle!" declared Clancy. "You're a life saver!" He bumped his coffee against the trader's coffee in good cheer.

A gnarled throaty chuckle from Umberto Allejandro Quinto filled the air. Max's cheeks glistened as she wept, and little Tyler's fists reached for the heavens as he shouted, "We're going home! Peanuts! Popcorn! And crackerjacks! Home at last! Home at last!"

Not easily spotted in this wonderful moment was Jack's breaking heart. He smiled brightly, courageously holding onto a mask of happiness, but deep inside he felt his adoration for Max tearing him apart. How could he possibly be with her back home? He fretted. Their love had yet to start—and it would soon be over.

Patting Clancy on the back, he tried swallowing the hurt. "Great news, huh, old boy?" He barely noticed the jolly face nodding back at him in response.

The trader spoke to the two men. "I would very much like to meet de Jean Harlow."

"Oh, boy!" Clancy agreed. "That would be something, wouldn't it?"

"Easy boys," warned Max, while her eyes awkwardly locked with Jack's. "Easy." She smiled fast and turned away.

"Let us feast!" the trader advised. He waved them on to follow.

"A feast too?" Clancy responded, hastily jumping on the Latino's heels, marching off with happy feet. "We've struck the jackpot! Yessiree!" While the merry band paraded onward, the copilot slapped Jack on the back. "The gods are surely smiling on us, eh, Jack? A happier day I cannot imagine."

Jack laughed as an actor playing a role and turned to Max. He saw her stare fall within herself and wished he knew what she was thinking.

*   *   *

Lounging in hammocks, warmed before a flickering fire, the stranded five had every reason to be content. Their bellies were full; they felt relatively safe—and they were going home.

"This has been good for me," said Clancy reflectively. Half his tired face smiled. He watched Chohnjo sleeping, still wearing a familiar, much too large cap.

"A good meal?" Jack responded.

"No." The copilot went on. "Being here. I wish it hadn't happened for your sakes, and I'll always feel bad about poor

Captain Horrigan. He lost his life and his beloved Goose on the same day. But, what I mean is … Well, look." Clancy held both hands in the air. "No shakes."

Tyler, baffled, asked, "What is it that was shaking you?"

"Stupidity mostly. Not appreciating what I had when I had it."

Still puzzled, Tyler blurted, "Is it stupid for me to wish I had ice cream?"

Jack brightened at the youngster's suggestion. "Say, wouldn't that be nice?"

"You two are still hungry?" asked Max.

"Well, for ice cream. Yeah."

Across the courtyard, with a cadre of Indians huddled among supplies, Umberto Allejandro Quinto puffed smoke into the night air from a long bamboo pipe. Amiable murmurs and chuckles were heard over the distance.

"Mr. Hunter," Lindy began. "You promised to show me the dancing from the ballroom scene in *Treasure of the Sahara Sky*."

Max softly interjected, "Lindy, I'm sure Mr. Hunter is much too tired—"

"On the contrary. It would be my privilege and pleasure, young lady." With some effort, Jack stood from his hammock and stepped out under the stars. "It was a waltz, if I remember correctly."

With an awkward mix of excitement and bashfulness, Lindy followed Jack. She let him raise one of her hands while he put her other on his shoulder. Her large blue eyes blinked into his, and her glasses caught a glint of fire.

"It helps when you're starting out to count in your head. One, two, three. One, two, three. One, two, three." He demonstrated, leading her forward, to the side then back. Slowly, clumsily, they swayed. Jack's dancing ability proved surprisingly confident and graceful, not unlike the finesse he displayed as a slapstick performer. "When it's comfortable, glide." He was patient with her, gentle and fatherly.

"It looks easy in the movies," she said.

"I owe a great deal to editors. And you're doing just fine, my dear." The handsome star guided her into a faster pace. "It would be easier if we had some music."

Hefting himself into a proud stance, Clancy said, "Perhaps I could hum something for you. I used to sing in a choir in my younger days. I even had the chance to solo once or twice." The copilot cleared his throat and, with a joyous tenor voice, charmed the night skies with a popular bouncy tune from not too many years earlier.

To fall in love
Is hopelessly wonderful
To fall in love
With you most of all
To fall in love
Is hopelessly marvelous
To fall in love
With you most of all

Jack laughed and declared with gusto, "Say, Clancy, you're pretty good! Keep singing!" Carving box steps into the hard earth, he gently whisked the eleven-year-old round and round in a tight embrace.

Increasingly embarrassed, Lindy eventually called to her aunt. "Auntie Max, you take over."

"Oh, no." Max punctuated her resistance with upturned hands.

"I can learn just as well from watching."

"Yeah," Jack said. "C'mon, Auntie Max. Don't be a spoilsport."

Max stood, making a big show of her reluctance. "Fine." As Lindy stepped aside, Max leisurely walked into the arms of Jack.

"You planned for this to happen," he said.

"Oh, here we go. Mister Ego."

Clancy resumed as if backed by a full orchestra.

JACK AND THE JUNGLE LION

To fall in love
Is hopelessly wonderful
To fall in love
With you most of all

With a sudden boom, bright light rained from high heavens. Fireworks—traded to the Indians—were lit and spraying illumination. Beaming native faces cried out with the flashes of radiance. For brief seconds at a time, night turned bright as day.

"No snide witticisms about my dancing, Miss Daniels?"

"I can think of a few." Her breath quickened from the strength of his grip around her waist. "But I thought the whole point of this was to offer an example of how it's supposed to be."

"So, you're *pretending* to enjoy this?"

"That's right," she said. The flirtatious sparkle in his eyes had not changed since the moment they met. Max fixed her eyes on his from inches away and felt her defensive façade falling.

"You're almost convincing. Maybe you should be an actress."

Her vulnerable expression reappeared as she asked, "Why didn't you marry the princess in *Treasure of the Sahara Sky*?"

"The idea was that I would earn the privilege of marrying her by locating a valuable jewel, missing for many years. But I didn't want her to marry me because of some jewel. I wanted her to marry me because she loved me."

"And I bet she did, didn't she? By the end?"

"Yes, she did," Jack said definitively. "Took her a while to realize it though."

Again, her stare fell within herself. This time, however, Jack had total confidence in his abilities to read her thoughts. "What I just said—that would have been a good cue for you to kiss me ... If we were pretending."

Max stiffened. "Well, we should stop. I think they can see how—"

"No." Jack strengthened his embrace of her. "C'mon, Miss Daniels, why do you want to run from this?"

"Because—" Her face reddened. Tears suddenly sparkled on long lashes, but her beautiful eyes did not waver. "You're married."

"I'm crazy about you."

"Please don't talk to me that way. I'm not like a film star who falls in and out of love so easily. I'm not—"

"I want to kiss you."

"Jack … I've never been in love."

"Then it makes sense why you're so awful at it."

"Don't tease me."

"Okay."

"Most men don't want an already-made family. Have you considered that? What about the children?"

"You're a hero to them. I'm not big enough to stand in the way of that. My only regret is that I wish I knew them sooner. I wish I knew you sooner."

Another flash of fireworks burst. Streaks of light soared upward into a booming and crackling night sky. It was beneath this shower of falling stars, with everyone watching, that Jack finally kissed Max.

CHAPTER THIRTEEN

Climbing above the soft green of the jungle, Umberto Allejandro Quinto's Staggerwing launched triumphantly into the morning sky. Slanting streams of violet hung in the orange heavens, and before long, the immense blue-green of the sea became the whole horizon.

As noon and afternoon passed, the rescued were cramped beyond capacity at a little over two hundred miles per hour. Jack's monkey refused to be left behind and cried the entire time they were in the air. Yet bravely they carried on, expressing eternal gratitude to the star-struck trader.

An evening passed in Iztapa, Guatemala, before they again trudged over latitude lines crossed previously when they bounced south.

Later, they landed again. Jack kissed the ground. He blessed the airport but loudly cursed the town they had returned to, calling the people liars and cheats—scoundrels who smile to your face while stabbing your back. When Max informed Jack they were in Mexico, he reddened with embarrassment and apologized profusely to the Latino employees. The trader quickly gassed up his Staggerwing, and they were soon revisiting clouds.

As night blanketed the western hemisphere, they slept, slumbering, snoring, whimpering in dreams while they were carried across sparkling black skies. Then finally, like a cluster of fairy dust in the far distance, Los Angeles came into view, twinkling brightly beyond a barren floor.

The tired, craggy face of Umberto Allejandro Quinto pointed and burst into song. "Hooray for Hollywood!" His passengers awoke, scrambled for a view, and roared with excitement. After several communiqués with the nightshift ground control, they descended.

At long last, they were home.

"Gee whiz! We almost didn't believe you!" a ground-crew member gushed.

"Great pleasure to know you're safe, Mr. Hunter!" added another.

"Are you sure there isn't something we can get for you, Mr. Hunter? We're all big fans of your pictures!"

Marching across the airstrip with his new best friends at his back, Jack graciously thanked the boys and said, "We requested cabs over the radio—"

"They're here, and with engines alive, Mr. Hunter!"

Reiterating deepest appreciation and fondest wishes, they each said goodbye to Umberto Allejandro Quinto. Max kissed him. Clancy shook his hand. He got big hugs from the children; then Jack pressed a key into the trader's palm and whispered, "The Garden of Allah. Sunset Boulevard. Bungalow five. Stay as long as you like."

"*Gracias, señor!*"

Gripping the bushy-haired man's arm, Jack sighed, "Thanks." They parted. A moment later, remembering something, Jack turned back to the man. "Oh, Umberto! Good luck with Jean Harlow! She'll be your neighbor!"

From the South American trader came a deep throaty chuckle. Thrusting his fists into the misty chill, he howled like a wild man and pounded his chest. A moment later, he quieted his lusty antics and waved a jolly goodbye.

*   *   *

Jack's residence—Lomond Manor—sat nestled atop a hill on a sleepy street. As the cab carrying Jack, Max, Clancy, and the kids rolled to a stop, they were silent, unsure, dulled by the shock of being home.

Lampposts, neatly aligned along the sidewalks, warmed the night. The moon cast sparkles on swaying palm leaves.

Jack got out of the passenger seat, shut the door, and walked around the car to an open back window. "The Yacht Club on Friday then?"

Max nodded.

"Everything's going to be peachy," he promised.

Leaping onto his head, Jack's mischievous white-faced capuchin gibbered with curiosity at the civilized world and bounded off into fresh-cut lawn, scrambling uphill, before disappearing into shadows.

Jack shook his head and reached into the cab, affectionately touching the children's tired faces. He smiled, reassuring them that all would be good.

"Goodnight, Jack," said Clancy with a wave.

The cab rolled away. Jack remained alone in the street, watching them go. Standing in tattered clothes, he turned to his home—looking strangely, uncomfortably lost.

He walked the palatial mansion's long driveway and then through a front door framed in ornate Renaissance-style stone. Inside, he left the lights dark, feeling some trepidation about reentering his previous life.

Behind him, he felt a presence. Whirling suddenly, he found a shadowy figure raising a golf club, ready to strike!

"Mr. Quigg?" he shouted.

"Mr. Hunter?"

Jack beamed. "Mr. Quigg, it is I!" The handsome star threw his arms to his sides, presenting himself for identification.

The elderly butler lowered the club and brightened a lamp, revealing a ragged, almost unrecognizable Jack Hunter. Genuine fondness moved the muscles of Mr. Quigg's face for perhaps the very first time. It was a subtle grin, but a grin nonetheless. "You are alive," he gasped. "Thank God."

"Very good to see you, Mr. Quigg."

"Oh, this is quite a relief. Whatever happened? I'll awaken Mrs. Lomond."

"You know she'll tear your head off or throw you out the window if you wake her."

Mr. Quigg hesitated, puzzled. "She should know you're all right, sir."

"Mr. Quigg, will you make me one of your famous sandwiches and share a beer with me in the kitchen?"

*   *   *

Having restored some of his famously polished appearance, Jack sat atop a high kitchen counter finishing a sandwich and glass of beer. Clothed in a silk robe and bloodied tuxedo trousers, he hardly spoke.

Seated at a table, Mr. Quigg interrupted the long silence. "Mrs. Lomond has started a new picture."

"Terrific. No point sitting around worrying about me."

"She's a very determined woman," Mr. Quigg said with a typically diplomatic flare.

"That she is," Jack agreed. "God bless her."

"God bless her."

The handsome star set aside his glass and plate. He could see neither the kitchen nor his butler, as his stare remained firmly fixated on his heart. "I've met someone else. I've fallen in love."

Mr. Quigg offered no response, not even a twitch.

"Any advice?"

"Mmm … difficult."

"Mr. Quigg …" Jack adopted a more demanding tone. "Man to man."

His elderly butler pondered the situation for several moments. Finally, he raised a chin and spoke with brutal candidness. "You've wasted years married to a self-obsessed, ungrateful windbag. For a man who can have anything, you've been an unbelievable fool. My advice: stop being a fool."

CHAPTER FOURTEEN

The next day, the California sun bounced off a lineup of motorcars parading down a modest street seeking curb space. Men in fedoras and holding notepads rushed toward a small home, followed by flashing cameras.

From within, Max opened a curtain. Worried as she peered outside, she saw press credentials on breast pockets and hatbands. Her doorbell rang, repeatedly.

"Hiya, Sam," one fast-footed man said to another.

"Whattaya say, Mickey?"

"Still workin' for that rag?"

"Coverin' the same malarkey that's on the radio."

Max opened her front door, confronting these men along with an approaching flock of similarly fashioned others. "I can't tell you anything. We were in the jungle. Now we're not. Good day."

As Max tried slamming her door, it was blocked with desperate quickness by one of the pressmen. "What was he like?" the man asked.

"Was it difficult to resist his charms?" demanded another.

"No!"

The one called Mickey grabbed a pencil from behind his ear, licked it and pressed it against his notepad. "Must have been exciting to find yourself living out the harrowing circumstances we usually associate with a Jack Hunter picture."

"He's not like the characters he plays in those daredevil, tough-guy movies," Max revealed. "In real life he's very silly. He's gentle. He's a goofball, and we came to appreciate him very much. He's fun and kind. Enough? It'll have to be, as I've nothing more to say. Good day, gentlemen."

Max slammed the door and punctuated it with a loud turning of the lock.

*   *   *

Meanwhile, in the upper reaches of Lomond Manor, Jack entered his wife's bedroom. Theda, arms draped with clothes, dashed from a walk-in closet to a dressing partition. A radio pitched fast words and music into the air.

"Jack! Darling!" exclaimed Theda. "I was told you'd returned safely. Thank God for that. I want to hear all about your travails, but they'll have to wait till tonight. I'm dreadfully late."

Before Jack could reply, Mr. Quigg appeared holding an ivory-colored French telephone attached to a far-reaching cord. "For Mr. Hunter," he announced.

Awkwardly shuffling his feet, Jack muttered to his wife, "I'm anxious to hear about your movie."

"I'd give you the book it's based on, but there are no pictures. And I know how you get confused when there are only words."

Mr. Quigg cleared his throat and said, "The head of the studio is inquiring about your well-being, sir."

Jack, wearing a crisp three-piece suit, took the handset and answered. "Hello, Louie."

"Jackie, my boy! I prayed every day you'd come back to us."

"Well, that's nice ..." The handsome star paced. "Now listen, Louie," he said. "About the picture we didn't get to—"

"Don't worry, Jack. Picture's in the can."

"Oh?" Jack stopped. His head raised in surprise. "I see. Well, whom did you replace me with?"

Alarmed, Theda paused with her fashion options, offering her husband a mask of compassion.

"Bickford."

"Bickford?"

"But he did it as a tribute to you."

"Of course he did. Well, maybe Hal Hartford and I—"

"Hartford directed the Bickford picture. They had a fabulous time. They're working on another right now."

"Hal's directing a new picture? With Charles Bickford? Right now?"

Holding the base of the telephone on a silver tray, Mr. Quigg kept up with Jack's rapid pacing

"Jack, don't make me feel bad. Put yourself in my shoes."

"I understand. You thought I was dead."

"And it was very sad."

"I appreciate that, Louie."

"I'm glad you're all right, Jack."

"Always a pleasure to hear your voice, Louie." Jack hung up the telephone and stood still. He massaged the lines in his face.

Mr. Quigg turned on his heels, exiting the bedroom.

"Jack! Darling!" Theda put a dramatic hand to her forehead. "I know exactly how you feel. I know that being out of work as an actor can seem like the death of God." She approached, placed a cold palm on his cheek and then hastened back to her partition, blurting, "Unemployment is the painful cross we must bear."

"Yes, well, I don't really care." With his head down, eyes brushing over fancy carpets from the Far East, Jack resumed pacing. "Theda, listen to me. What I'm about to say is important. I'm not sure how you'll take this, but I think in the long run—"

While Jack nervously spoke, his wife crossed from her partition to her bathroom without notice. She turned on a faucet.

"In the long run you'll thank me for changing the direction of our lives." Jack stopped ambulating across the carpets and stood with legs braced, determination tightening his jaw—facing Theda with his back. "I've met someone," he admitted. "And I want to be with her. I need to be with her."

The faucet turned off. Theda returned from her bathroom to behind her partition. While tossing undergarments and dresses over the panels, she said nothing.

Jack turned—awaiting her wildly theatrical reaction. "Did you hear what I said?"

The silent film queen popped her head out from behind her screen and lied. "Of course I did."

"I think it's best for both of us, don't you?"

"It's very considerate. Very thoughtful. And I'm very late." She stepped out from behind the partition wearing a stunning bead and feather dress while holding another made of satin and diamonds. "Which dress looks more expensive?"

"Uh—"

"Never mind. I'm late."

Jack held up a finger, about to respond, when Theda suddenly launched back into her messy jumble of clothing. Just then, something on the radio caught Jack's attention; Walter Winchell began broadcasting, speaking in his familiar staccato style, tapping out words with the rat-a-tat speed of a machine.

Having heard his name, Jack raised the volume on the radio.

"That's right—not dead, as feared to be! Movie star Jack Hunter, back from the Amazon! And before you ask, 'How could the real Jack Hunter survive any place without champagne, caviar, and a beautiful woman?' Well, he didn't have to! The very lovely Maxine Daniels—said to be on her way to work in a behind-the-scenes capacity for the same picture—survived with the handsome hero! When asked what the real Jack Hunter was like, she described him as silly and a big goofball! When asked if she found the Saturday matinee idol charming, she said, 'No!' You have to wonder what happened between those two! In other news—"

Jack turned off the radio.

Bounding out from behind the partition, exiting the bedroom in a satin dress and high heels, Theda said to Jack, "Get some rest, will you? Your face looks even more blank than usual."

* * *

Across town, Max also turned off the Walter Winchell report. She stood speechless. Her insides tightened. Biting down on a thumbnail, her face filled with fret. "Shucks," she finally said.

From the noiseless radio, she looked to her frayed couch. Tyler and Lindy sat with long faces, chins dropped. Little Tyler held a pillow in his lap, unable to lift his disappointed eyes to Auntie Max.

Lindy looked up and said, "I hope Mr. Hunter didn't hear that. Did he ever mention whether or not he listens to Walter Winchell?"

Max paced, arms crossed, shaking her head, trying to figure out how to escape such a fix.

CHAPTER FIFTEEN

Jack's white-faced capuchin sat on a couch, wearing a wool suit, looking terribly depressed. With forlorn eyes, he scratched his head and sighed.

The monkey was mimicking Jack, who believed himself the loneliest man on the planet. With hair disheveled and face unshaven, Jack dropped his hands into the pockets of his silk robe as he slowly paced. He looked at a clock on his mantle.

His fateful reunion with Max waited at the other end of the hour. He needed to dress, shave, and comb his hair, but he couldn't forget her mockery of him to the press. It would have been one thing to say mean things to his face, but to say mean things about him to reporters was quite another! He had a successful career as a film star, a reputation to uphold!

"She thinks I'm a goof," he said to the capuchin.

The monkey nodded in response.

Suddenly, the telephone rang. Jack answered, "Hello."

Theda, with her remarkably disciplined diction, barked frustration at Jack through the line. "I'm finished, and Mr. Quigg is not here! What are you doing?"

"Thinking about going to the Yacht Club."

"An excellent idea. It's Friday. They're having that big party."

"Party?"

"We'll have a lovely time."

"Theda, don't you remember what we talked about?"

"Everybody will be there, Jack. It will be delightful."

"What about your Friday night Seduce the World meetings? With your agent and press agent and—"

"Irving is sick. We're postponing."

"But, Theda, it's a Seduce the World meeting! Is this how you seduce the world? One guy's absent and so—"

"Mr. Quigg has arrived! I'll meet you at the Yacht Club! Please be prompt! Unlike your horrendous butler!"

Jack could almost hear her telephone slamming as the line died. He turned to his monkey who sat despairingly with his head in his hands.

*　　　*　　　*

Inside the ritzy and packed California Yacht Club, a big band jumped with their best Tommy Dorsey-era swing. Visible through the windows, schooners and speedboats bobbled on the Pacific.

As Jack anxiously searched for Max, waiters zipped through fast-moving crowds collecting tips. Cleaned up and dashing, he sported a slim-fitted suit. He looked everywhere for her, continuously coming up empty.

Champagne bottles and lobster plates covered a sea of snow-white tablecloths. A double boiler, brimming with creamy chocolate for dipping strawberries, took up the center of the main room.

Spectacularly grand as ever, Theda entered.

"I lied. I admit it." Irving, a short bald man with smart spectacles, put on a pleading face as Theda stormed at him.

"Did you also lie to get yourself into this party?" she lashed at him through tightening lips.

"I thought you'd go on with the Seduce the World meeting without me!"

Jack nervously watched his wife berate her weasel of a press agent while wondering what happened to Max. Had she arrived and gone? Where could she be?

"Jack!"

The shout of his name had the anxious star almost leaping from his shoes. He turned to Louie who stood before a cadre of sycophants—including two Louie-loyalists Jack despised the most, Alexander and Nate.

"Jack," the studio boss repeated. "I've got an idea for your next picture." His swaggering manner and giggling sidekicks pointed to a joke yet to be told. "You're tied to the train tracks, crying and screaming like a sissy. You wet your pants. But then, from out of nowhere, just in a nick of time, a dame rushes in, unties you, picks you up and carries you off to safety!"

Red in the face, shaking with hilarity, Alexander—looking remarkably similar to Jack—stood behind Louie. "And then you look up at her and say, 'Ah, my heroine!'" Another round of machine-gun laughter blasted the action hero.

Jack smiled calmly in the face of their roaring mockery and said to Alexander, "It makes you crazy that you're not me, doesn't it?" As a waiter passed, Jack snatched a glass of champagne from a tray. "I learned a fascinating trick from the tribesman of the Amazon," he told them.

Knocking back the bubbly, Jack swished it around in his mouth then aggressively spit it into Alexander's face, sending it out into a great spray, showering the dandified toady. "It's just something they do." Jack smiled. "Charming, isn't it?"

While Louie's jaw dropped in shock, Alexander found a napkin for his face and pinched the stinging alcohol from his eyes. Recovering, he furiously looked up to find Jack vanished.

Outside the California Yacht Club, an evening sun blazed on the horizon. Wearing makeup and a slinky, hip-hugging dress, Max clopped up the steps to the entrance. She put a gloved hand to the small hat perched to one side of her head, fidgeted a little and took a sharp breath before marching into the lobby.

A male host in a white jacket called to her as she passed. "Excuse me. Stop right there, please."

Max turned.

"Sorry, ma'am. Tonight is a members-only affair."

"I'm here to meet Jack Hunter. He's one of your members."

Exuding an air of haughty condescension, the host said, "Okay, he didn't mention it to me, which would be the normal thing for him to do."

"Well, he's a little slow. Perhaps he forgot."

"There is a movie house down the street playing one of his pictures. If you really want to see him, I would suggest you go there."

Irving desperately trailed Theda, bursting from the main room into the lobby. "Darling, we'll reschedule for Sunday at my place! We'll make it a champagne brunch!"

"You! In the white jacket!" Theda howled at the host. "I demand that you remove this disgraceful turtle of a man from the party!" She pointed at Irving, who couldn't stop biting his fingers.

"All right, there you go," the host said to Max, who was shocked by the presence of Theda Lomond. "You've caught your first glimpse of a movie star. Now move along."

In the next instant, Jack came barreling into the lobby, seeing his wife, then Max. He rushed to the one he loved, as though he hadn't seen her in years. "I didn't ask for her to come," he explained.

Recognizing that Max had been truthful about being Jack's guest, the host turned his conceited nose, masking his embarrassment.

Several feet away, Theda yelled at Irving, "There are hundreds—if not thousands!—in line to fill your shoes!"

Regarding the explosive scene created by Theda Lomond and the bald man, Max said to Jack, "She doesn't look too devastated over the fact that you left her, or doesn't she know that yet?"

Finally, Alexander charged into the lobby, veins popping with extreme dislike. Quickly locating Jack, he expressed hostility in a manner befitting his high-society status. "Excuse me! Mr. Hunter! I really don't appreciate what you did back there!"

Jack retorted calmly. "Your envy of me is really starting to make you look bad. You should keep a safe distance. You'll compare better that way."

The mogul's minion surprised Jack by lunging for him, grabbing him by the lapel and shoving him into a wall.

Rushing to intervene was the host. "Please! Please! No fighting!"

Irving tossed his drink into his own face, crying to Theda, "There! Feel better?"

"Only a little," she replied with a dismissive gesture.

Another dapper man with a high-and-mighty attitude approached Max with curious eyes. "I'm Nate. I don't believe we—"

"Maxine Daniels," she snapped. "Nice to meet you."

"From the radio broadcast? How very interesting."

Loud and intoxicated, fattening the crowded lobby further, Louie crashed through the door. "What the heck is everybody doing in the lobby?"

After a few moments of physical struggle with each other, Alexander released his grip on Jack. "I guess you don't really need further embarrassment, do you, Jack?"

"C'mon!" Louie bellowed. "Any average Joe can stand around in the lobby!"

Somewhat reluctantly, the hostility-fueled crowd followed Louie into the main room decorated for dining and dancing. The brass section struck sweeping blows over pounding drums, raising the volume of voices in conversation. The decibel level was startling.

Regaining composure and distancing himself from his obvious enemies, Jack placed a tender hand on Max's back.

When Theda caught sight of the affectionate gesture, her nostrils flared and penciled eyebrows hit the ceiling. Her cold blood quickly boiled.

Snickers and whispers passed between Nate and Alexander. Covering their lips, they breathed tidbits into the ears of others. Gossip spread like wildfire among the hoity-toity handmaidens and slaves of Babylonian depravity. Fingers began pointing at Jack and Max between giggling fits.

"Why haven't you told her, Jack?" Max demanded to know.

"I did tell her!"

The perceived degeneracy on the part of Jack Hunter, coupled with the public insult to yesteryear's glamour queen, encouraged greater excitement among the already delirious guests.

Oblivious to the outrage he caused, Jack snipped at Max. "Listen to the radio much?"

"I used to," she responded. "Then I decided all the music was overly sentimental and phony—like you! It's humiliating for me to be here, and it's your fault! Everyone's looking at me like I'm the mistress!"

"I wasn't even sure you'd come—"

"Obviously!"

"I thought you might have gone back to the way you felt when we first met."

"What I said was taken out of context."

"What was the context? Was it the *I Hate Action Hero Hour* or something?"

Leading with a half-crazed smile, Theda swooped in, interrupting the intimate bickering. "Jack, introduce me to your friend."

Lines of concern deepened on Jack's face. "Uh—this is Max. Maxine Daniels. She was with me on the airplane. And then in the jungle."

"Oh," muttered Theda. She looked at Max. "Did you forget your autograph or something?"

Without batting an eye, Max returned fire. "I'm sorry. I know you're Jack's wife, but I forget your name."

Theda clearly had not anticipated trading insults with one who could retaliate. While the surface of her disposition revealed only a subtle modification, there appeared to be a more pronounced transformation within her—something similar to that of a melting witch.

Instinctively, without knowing why he did so, Jack tried soothing the contentiousness. "Max, this is *Theda Lomond*."

Max shrugged as if the name meant nothing. "Oh?"

Theda's flesh quivered and eyes bulged into something hideous. Witnessing a brand-new expression on his wife's face, Jack was tempted to telephone the California State Hospital for the Insane. A psychologically damaged operatic outburst was noticeably imminent.

"She is?" Louie's drunken shout stole everyone's attention. "I wanna meet her! Point her—point her out to me! Where's she?"

Pointing, Alexander exclaimed, "The one with the lost puppy look on her face!"

All heads turned to Max.

"I find it impossible to believe Jack had an affair with this woman!" Theda dramatically proclaimed for all to hear. "If he had he would have provided her with something sophisticated to wear!" As the crowd laughed, the silent film star's chin jutted out and saucer-sized eyes glared.

Following Theda's cue, Alexander now took his turn at denigrating Jack's guest. "Jack, buy her some proper jewelry so she doesn't stand out so much!"

While these gleeful eruptions burst, Max seemed to be physically shrinking before their harsh judgment. She wished she could disappear, run and hide, but what pride remained held strong.

Jack stepped away from Max. Smiling, he strolled past Alexander toward a display of assorted pies. Deciding that the coconut cream would make for the most effective weapon of the bunch, he lifted it off a tray and turned back toward Alexander.

Alexander crossed his arms defiantly, silently daring Jack.

The couple hundred Yacht Club guests began pounding on tables, chanting, "Do it! Do it! Do it!"

Without hesitation, the handsome star lunged forward, launching it.

But Alexander ducked. The pie flew over him, passing with dynamic speed—

And smashing smack dab into Max's face, knocking her back on her heels. Stunned, she stood with whipped cream and crust falling off her pained expression and down her dress. Stumbling around, she wiped the dessert from her eyes, surrounded by a savage roar of laughter.

Jack's hands covered his mouth in horror. What had he done? "Max, wait!" he cried, as she bounded for the exit.

While Jack wasn't looking, Alexander grabbed the large kettle full of creamy chocolate, hoisted it over the star's head, and dumped it over him. Guests rolled on the floor, holding their aching stomachs, desperately trying to calm their laughter.

Jack made a sudden charge for Alexander but slipped in the spilled chocolate, crashing down on the hardwood floor.

Theda—who never, ever laughed—struggled to speak between giggling fits. "That wretched monkey you brought home is smarter than you, Jack! And composes himself with more dignity!"

Once Jack stood, Alexander socked him hard in the face, dropping him back onto the flooring. Relishing the attention, Alexander thrust his fists in the air as a boxer after a winning bout.

Slithering in chocolate, Jack managed to kick his nemesis behind a knee, causing him to stumble and fall. Jack leapt atop Alexander and unleashed a pounding of brutal blows to his face.

Outside the California Yacht Club, Max marched to her car, still wiping pie from her face. Sobbing, she removed her keys from her purse. She fumbled with them, and they fell to the pavement. Her car suffered a swift kick resulting from her terrible frustration.

Jack hurried into the street, desperately searching for Max. His nose bled. His suit was torn and covered in chocolate. With twilight upon them, he couldn't see much.

He spotted a car down the road. Brake lights flared.

"Max?"

She motored toward the western sea, into the last bit of light from the day.

CHAPTER SIXTEEN

Louie sat captivated behind an opulent black and gold desk as Tyler and Lindy played out melodramatic scenes before him. His enormous office was carved out in art-deco décor, from the lavish lamps to the terracotta sunburst above the fireplace.

Lindy addressed her brother in a tomboy voice and put a cold shoulder between them. "We decided it would be nice if you were handsome," she said. "And so the only thing we could think to do about it was to paint your face." Bending forward, she mimed painting on her brother's face.

Then, with a sudden burst of energy, Tyler leapt around the office, snarling and pointing invisible arrows at his sister.

Lindy's big blue eyes widened. She reacted to Tyler by feigning great fear, straightening herself, pretending to be tied and gagged.

"I'll save you!" Tyler bellowed. His chest puffed out. He jumped before her, daring imaginary enemies to come forward and fight.

"And then we used a platter as a shield," Lindy explained to the studio boss in her own voice. "Oh, no!" she exclaimed, acting again. "The shield's been hit with a fire arrow!"

Tyler grabbed the invisible shield and threw it against the invisible wall. He flailed his arms and, with his little mouth, made the sounds of a roaring fire. "It's the wall of fire!"

"The wall of fire!" Lindy repeated to Louie.

Enthralled, Louie put nervous fingers to his face. He watched Tyler take Lindy by the hand and bound—without hesitation—straight through the make-believe flames.

"And then there was dancing," Lindy announced. She positioned Tyler's stance, and around the room they waltzed.

"I'm crazy about you," Tyler said.

Lindy—believing her role far more complicated than her brother's—hammed it up. "Please don't talk to me that way," she exclaimed in a breathy voice. "I'm not like a film star who falls in and out of love so easily." She batted her eyelashes at him.

"I want to kiss you."

"Jack," she sighed. "I have never been in love."

Tears streamed down Louie's fat cheeks. He leapt out of his chair and declared, "Beautiful! It's an epic!"

Outside Louie's office, his pretty secretary sat pounding away at a typewriter. Pacing across the room, with a new hat in his hands, was Clancy.

The big door burst open. Louie caught their attention, pointed at his secretary. "Get me Jack Hunter and that animal dame!"

"Already telephoned them, sir."

Beaming, Louie next pointed at Clancy and said, "Boy, oh boy! And I thought I was doing you a favor!"

*   *   *

Flanked by soundstages, a little guard gate protected the factories of fun and illusion from real-world infiltration, and for many years the same friendly man with a badge stood within this guard gate keeping a watchful eye on the wide boulevard outside.

A silver convertible roadster announced its approach with a blaring horn sounding like the delirious cry of a sick goose. The guard smiled brightly as it drew near.

"Hiya, Jack! Been a while!"

Jack steadied his rumbling roadster. "Still keeping an eye on the funny farm, are you, Joe?"

"Yes, sir. Say, your ex-wife came in a while ago."

"Oh, yeah? What's she working on?"

"I hear the picture takes place on the moon, and she plays an alien dictator who speaks a strange language through her nose."

"Nice to know I still have some influence at this studio."

"Folks have missed you, Jack."

"Thanks, Joe. Great to see you."

Moments later, Jack strolled briskly through the studio's decorative halls, looking sharp, whistling all the way. Eventually, he rounded a corner and saw another old friend. "Clancy!"

The tubby copilot bounded forward with a sprightly step and jolly face. He shook Jack's hand with gusto. "How are you, Mr. Hunter?"

"Well, I'm all right. What are you doing here?"

"Oh, uh, remember there was some talk with the head of the studio before we took off? Some talk of a favor—"

"That's right. I remember. Say, Clancy, are you going to be around for a bit? I'm terribly late for a meeting."

"I'll be right here, Mr. Hunter."

"Call me Jack," the handsome star said while entering Louie's office. Stunned to see who had been waiting for him inside, his face dropped.

Ravishing as ever, Max looked up at him.

"Come on in, Jack. Have a seat," demanded Louie.

Jack slowly closed the door but remained standing. "Miss Daniels," he muttered with a polite nod.

"Mr. Hunter."

"All right, you two," said Louie. "I brought you both here because I think your story would make for a fantastic picture." Seated behind his beautifully polished desk, Louie clipped a cigar, popped it in his big mouth, struck a match, and lit it. "I need details," he puffed. "Tell me about first contact with the headhunters."

"Oh, well, uh—" Jack faltered, lowering his eyes to the carpet. "I guess—I guess we were first alerted to their presence when—"

"Jack fell in a hole."

"Fell in a hole?" Louie questioned.

"Filled with poison-dipped thorns," Max added.

Louie scribbled notes with a cloud of smoke rising above him. "Poison-stick pit. That's great."

Jack and Max swapped quick awkward glances at each other.

"When did the romance begin?" Louie blurted.

At the opposite end of the room, a huge freestanding cabinet opened slightly. From within, two little spies peeked out— Tyler and Lindy.

"There wasn't any romance, really," said Max.

"There was a kiss," Jack nudged.

"But it was very innocent. In front of everyone. No big deal."

"Things were said—"

"And quickly forgotten."

Discouraged, Jack plopped into the empty chair next to Max. "I guess she knows what happened better than I do."

"Let's talk about casting," Louie snapped. "Jack, I know you're not working because of divorce proceedings, and you're buying a new residence outside Hollywood. Who do you think would be right? Errol Flynn's available."

"Flynn would be good," Jack concurred.

"Miss Daniels? Any ideas?"

Max no longer looked at Louie. Her eyes fell inward, staring at emotions she had never felt before. She trembled. "Clark

Gable," she finally mumbled as if she had marbles in her mouth. She seemed desperate to revive her familiar self.

"Gable's more serious," Jack said.

"Yeah."

Louie shifted in his chair, considered Miss Daniels carefully, and then asked, "What about an actress playing you? What would she be like?"

For a minute, Louie received no reply.

"Miss Daniels?"

Her breathing quickened and brow furrowed. "I think perhaps foolish."

Louie also knotted his forehead, seeing Miss Daniels as a very odd duck. He waved his cigar at Jack, asking, "Jack, any ideas?"

"Well, the actress would have to be someone very beautiful, clever, funny, courageous, a loving mother." Jack saw tears well in Max's eyes; she rummaged through her purse for a hanky. "Emotional," he went on. "Stubborn."

Max gave Jack a swift kick to the leg.

"Violent."

"Violent?" repeated Louie. "Interesting."

From an intercom on Louie's desk came the petite voice of his secretary. "Wallace Beery says the rubber dragon doesn't look real."

Louie hammered down a fast fist. "Prima Donna bastard! I gotta go take care of this! Stay here!"

Clamping his cigar between his teeth, he stormed out, closing the door behind him—but not all the way. Quickly, Clancy's eyes combined with Louie's, and together they became a second party of scheming spies.

For a while, the world turned slowly, uneasily. Not knowing what to say, Max stood and stepped away from Jack. She wrung her hands, fidgeting—trying to hold herself together.

Afraid of being caught, Tyler and Lindy closed the cabinet door and listened as Jack divulged a carefully kept, most surprising secret—

"Jack Hunter's not my real name."

"Oh?" Max turned back to him.

"It's, um—it's Richard."

"Your name is Richard?"

"Uh-huh."

"Richard what?"

"Kublicky—Richard Kublicky."

"Ricky Kublicky?" Max let the name spin around her precious head a few times. "That's not such a bad name. It's a nice name."

Jack stood. He cut the space between them. "As I say it out loud, it occurs to me—it's going to take an extraordinary woman to say, 'Ricky Kublicky, I love you.'"

Max lifted her sparkling eyes into his and said, "Ricky Kublicky, I … heard of a movie where this silly, rogue of a character wants to marry this princess, but only if she loves him for who he is instead of for the things he's done."

"It's a familiar story. What happens?"

"It takes her a while … but not because of some long-missing jewel or because she doesn't know him well enough but because … she's scared."

Jack took her face in his hands. "I'll protect you."

She kissed him. "I've really missed you, Jack Hunter," she cried. "Or whatever your name is." They kissed again.

Triumphant shrieks of joy blasted down the doors. Tyler and Lindy jumped around as Clancy and Louie offered congratulatory handshakes and hugs to Jack and Max, who never looked so happy.

As anxious nerves settled and choking emotions were wiped from faces, Jack led Max, Clancy, and the kids around the studio. They walked among massive soundstages, surrounded by bustling workers—some driving golf carts, some riding bicycles. They passed spacemen and monsters, revolutionary war heroes and cowboys.

They passed Jack's white-faced capuchin, who offered them a fast wave.

"What's he doing here?" asked Max.

"He seemed bored, so I got him a job as a writer. This business—it's who you know."

When they came upon a painted backdrop of a sunset, Max asked, "Mr. Hunter, would you ride off into the sunset with us?"

"Nothing would give me greater pleasure, Miss Daniels." Jack reached out and wrapped his knuckles against the hard wood backdrop. "Better not use this one, though."

Unable to resist, they kissed again.

*   *   *

Mr. Quigg entered a rustic bedroom and drew the curtains. A blast of sunshine brightened a bed where the matinee idol slept crumpled among bundles of sheets and pillows.

Jack grumbled.

Suddenly, a big dog rushed in, leapt upon the bed, and licked Jack's face.

Still in pajamas, Tyler followed the big dog, pulling him off the bed and out of the room.

As they left, a Bengal tiger entered.

Mr. Quigg pondered the black and orange beast without a speck of emotion, while Jack remained unmoving under pillows.

Lindy, with a book under her arm, raced in and guided the tiger out.

Max entered, yawning. She carried two coffee cups and lured Jack out of bed with the promise of one.

As Mr. Quigg went about his day, Jack and Max, still in their nighttime silks, stepped outside, where Clancy could be seen in the distance, feeding a baby goat with a bottle.

Clancy whistled a familiar tune.

As Jack and Max breathed in the morning air and looked out at the wide-open land around their ranch, they could hear Clancy trade his whistling for words.

To fall in love
Is hopelessly marvelous
To fall in love
With you most of all

ABOUT STEPHEN JARED

As an actor Stephen Jared has appeared in numerous feature films, television series, and television commercials. His writings have appeared in various publications. He lives in Pasadena, California.